WAHIDA CLARK PRESENTS

Baltimore Raw

A Novel By

AISHA HALL

Wahida Clark Presents Publishing

60 Evergreen Place

Suite 904A

East Orange, New Jersey 07018

1(866)-910-6920

www.wclarkpublishing.com

Library of Congress Cataloging-In-Publication Data:

Aisha Hall

Baltimore Raw

ISBN 13-digit 9781944992590 (paper)

ISBN 13-digit 9781944992651 (ebook)

ISBN 13-digit 9781944992637 (Hardcover)

LCCN: 2019943686

1. Sex - 2. Lies - 3. Infidelity - 4. African American- HIV –

5. Homosexuality - 6. Violence - 7. Relationships

Cover design and layout by Nuance Art, LLC

Book design by www.artdiggs.com

Edited by Linda Wilson

Proofreader Rosalind Hamilton

Printed in USA

Baltimore Raw

CHAPTER 1

Von

Her wardrobe and shoe collection were so extensive, it took up an entire bedroom-sized walk-in closet. But all those expensive clothes could not satisfy the pain that clamped itself around her heart. So she decided to downsize. She began cutting up her own shit like a madwoman.

Sobbing, she destroyed things that were at one time her prized possessions. She shook her head over and over again, as black tears ran down her cheeks, making her look almost as grim as she felt. Then she heard footsteps running up the staircase, followed by her bedroom door flying open.

"Von! Where are you, girl?" It was her best friend Paige. Paige had been blowing up Von's phone and did not get an answer. So she rushed over to see what was going on. Opening the closet door, Paige discovered Von sitting on the floor in a pile of cut up clothes.

"Girl, what the hell are you doing? Are you crazy! Is

that your Chanel dress over there?" She hadn't taken the time to look at Von's face. She was too shocked by the sight in front of her. Von dropped the scissors and put her head between her trembling brown hands. Her cries stabbed against Paige like a dull knife. She squat down in front of her friend and raised her chin. "Oh God! What's wrong, Von? Talk to me!" she said sitting beside her and immediately hugging her.

Von's normally freshly manicured fingernails were broken and chipped. This was not her style at all. Von was a fly chick. She had thick black hair, cut into a long bob. She always looked pretty and perfect—the opposite of how she looked right now.

"You gotta talk to me, Von. Please tell me what's going on," Paige asked in a concerned tone.

"Oh God!" Von said with more tears and even more sobs.

"It's gonna be okay. Whatever it is. We've been through every possible thing ever since we were little girls. Whatever it is, I promise you, it will be okay." She wiped her best friend's tears. The television was loud, drowning out some of Von's sobs. Neither one of the girls paid attention to the report, which talked about Baltimore's body count already being 10 percent higher than it was last year. Paige got up and muted the television. Then she pulled her friend to her feet, and the two of them walked over to Von's plush bed. They both backed up until their backs were supported by Von's plush brown leather headboard.

Von pushed Paige's hands away from her face and jumped off the bed to her feet.

"It's *not* going to be all right! It's not! I'm too young to die so early. Too young, Paige!" she screamed.

"Von what the hell are you talking about? Is somebody after you?"

"No! It's Rodney's fault! I trusted him. That lying, cheating, no-good bastard! He gave me HIV! I got fucking AIDS! That bitch-ass nigga was running around fucking them damn fiends . . . stankin'-ass freaks! Anybody with a hole!" Von paused and wiped her tears away. That same hand appeared to be dipped in diamonds. She was rockin' a diamond bracelet, a gold Rolex, and a giant rock sitting atop a platinum ring—all gifts from the man who she felt had signed her death certificate.

"Oh my God!" is all that Paige could say. She fought back against her emotions, trying to avoid adding to the river of tears that had accumulated in the room already.

"All this fuckin' time . . . He's been out doing me dirty." She shook her head. "I swear to God, Paige, I wish I never met that piece of shit." Paige put her cream-colored hand on Von's honey-brown arm. The contrast had never been more obvious. Paige was about five-six, and Von was taller, about five-eight, with nothing shy of a model figure.

"Girl, you are not going to die. Stop talking like that.

Don't you know about the medicine they have these days? You can live a long and normal life," Paige said squeezing Von in a tight embrace. Von did not hug her back.

"I should give this shit to every no-good Tom, Dick, and Harry in the city." The anger in Von's voice stunned Paige. She knew her friend, and she *never* talked like this. Scared that Von might be serious, Paige looked her in the eyes and pointed her finger in her face.

"Now hold up, boo. You are trippin'. I know that is the anger in you speaking. You don't mean that. That shit is dead wrong. You are hurt and upset. We're going to see the best doctors and make sure you get the best care. We will get through this together."

Von's face dropped. Both of them had seen what AIDS had done to Baltimore. It had the highest rate in the country and the numbers were scary. Having unprotected sex in their city could be a death wish. They'd heard people say it, but to see it so up close and personal was beyond disheartening.

It was devastating.

"I thought about it, Paige. I don't want to go out like this. I always said if I ever found myself in a situation that might end my life, I would rather end it myself."

"Girl, are you crazy? Shut up talking like that. You are *only* 18 years old. You have plenty of life to live."

"No, for real. I think I'll just kill myself. Yeah, that's what I'll do."

"No! What you're gonna do is get off that bed and help me get your stuff back on the hangers and hanging back up in the closet. I gotta save the rest of this expensive shit."

"I don't care about none of that shit. Rodney bought it for me."

"So what? Don't cut up your shit."

"And you know what else, Paige . . . I don't think that muthafucka even *knows* he's sick. He's a walking infector."

"Mm mm mm! Girl! Maybe we should just wait until he comes in here tonight, and shoot him in the dick!" Paige said.

"Good idea!" And then the two of them fell out laughing.

"But seriously, Von, you have been there for me and Marla in a way I can never thank you enough for. My own mother didn't want to accept me and my 16-year-old pregnant self. You have been a great godmother to my daughter. And she's getting ready to have a big fourth birthday party. I need you there. So, if you're gonna kill yourself, do it after the party, bitch." Von started laughing, and the two of them fell out again. Then suddenly, Paige stopped laughing and looked at her friend. "I love you, Von. We are going to get through this. I promise."

"Thank you, friend. Well . . . Really, you are more like my sister."

"Man, Nasty is going to flip out."

Von's eyes widened with fear. "No! He will never know. I am *not* going to tell Nasty. Girl, are you crazy. My brother would lose his mind. I would not put his on him. Promise me you will never tell him."

"I promise, okay, okay. Calm down."

"You know how he is," Von said.

"I know. Okay, so where is Rodney's ass now?" Paige asked.

"I don't know."

"Well, he's probably running around with that young 16 -year-old girl. Her name's Star."

"Star? What are you talking about?" Paige put her head down. "So that rumor *is* true?"

"Look, Von, he's been creeping with her for a while. And I didn't want to tell you. I didn't wanna be the one to destroy your happiness."

"No, instead, you sat there and allowed that bitch-ass clown to destroy my life," Von spat. The truth struck Paige like a hot iron. The last thing she wanted to do was hurt her friend, and she ended up hurting her anyway. Von had been hurt her entire life. Her parents were Baltimore royalty before there was a hit put out on them when Von was just 9 years old. They were both murdered by cold-blooded killers. But those hitters were never found, and their deaths went unaccounted for. They left behind Von and her brother, Nasty.

"Von, come on. It's not like that, and you know it."

"I know that I got fucked over by him. I know it came from him having sex with a bunch of other women. How do I know that she wasn't the one who gave it to him? And that had I known about them messing around, I might have been able to get out of this relationship."

Paige didn't say anything. But they both knew that even if Von had known, she would not have left Rodney. It was just one of those situations that females find themselves in when they are so strung out over a man that they lose themselves. And that's what happened to Von.

"Just accept it. You're part of the reason why I'm sick now."

"I love you, Von. You know this. And I know you're upset. So I'm going to leave and come back tomorrow."

"Yeah, do that!" she spat with venom dripping from her tongue. Paige stepped out of the house, and Von slammed the door behind her. Paige's body jerked with the slamming of the door. It felt like a smack in the face. As she walked to her car tears fell from her eyes. Her friend's pain was her pain, and Von was right. Maybe if she'd said something, Von may have not gotten sick.

In the house, Von sat on the white velvet couch in her living room and opened up the day's mail. She got a letter from her brother, Nasty. Nasty had taken care of her after their parents got killed. She was 9, and Nasty was 13. They came home from school to find their parents dead. Nasty, being too smart for his own good, ran to the neighbors' house. His best friend Soulja lived across the street. Soulja snuck Nasty and Von in his house and hid them out for days.

Soulja's mother, Tilda, let them stay with her. She was no stranger to the dangers of street life. There was no guarantee that whoever killed their parents might come back to finish off the job. So Soulja's family protected Nasty and Von. And they became siblings in every sense of the word.

Even though Nasty was only 13, he took his job as Von's big brother extremely seriously. So did Soulja. They were obsessed with protecting her, and they were good at it. One time a boy touched Von's butt, and Soulja and Nasty viciously whipped his ass. He vowed to protect her with his life.

Growing up without parents, Nasty stayed in the streets. He wanted his little sister to have the best of the best. So he started robbing niccas. Nasty and Soulja would do whatever was necessary to keep money in their pockets, and they gained a reputation for being young and ruthless.

Nasty was consumed by anger over his parents and had damn near lost respect for people—period. He seemed to hate anybody who wasn't Von or Soulja. Years later, Nasty

AISHA HALL WITH WEEDIE

and Soulja became notorious drug dealers in Baltimore. The two of them were young teenagers, but they were moving more weight than seasoned, grown-ass men. At the age of 18, Nasty and Soulja had tracked down Nasty and Von's parents' killers in Brazil. The two got passports and made their way to Brazil with a guide. It was Soulja's Brazilian baby mother, Teja, who put them onto what she heard had happened. She was almost 30 when she got pregnant by a teenager. But he was more man than any other men she'd ever met.

While they were gone, Nasty left Von in the care of his man Rodney. Rodney had promised to look out for young Von while they were gone. But Nasty and Soulja had no idea how much of a snake Rodney really was.

When Soulja and Nasty got back from their trip, the feds were waiting for them. They were arrested at the airport. The two of them got stuck in prison, and young Von got stuck with Rodney.

CHAPTER 2

Rodney placed the tip of his rolled up $50 bill to the line of raw dope that was sitting on a hand-sized mirror and sniffed until the line disappeared. He let his head fall back as he squeezed his nose, followed by a sniff to make sure he got his whole issue. The bathroom was cozy, with heated marble tiles and plush floor rugs. He was a flashy dude.

He kept several cribs. And that was expected for a man like him who always had so much going on in the streets. In his bedroom was a young teen who should have had her ass in school but was more interested in fucking around with a dope dealer. She thought that gave her some type of status. It gave her status, all right.

"Your phone has been ringing off the hook. You better come and get it before I answer it," Kia said. He yelled at her from behind the closed bathroom door.

"That'll be the last phone you pick up because I'd chop your gottdamn hands off and feed 'em to my gator," he responded. Kia looked at the receiver and decided that it wouldn't be a good idea to test Rodney. Just as she put the phone down, he stepped in the room with water dripping from his nostrils. His eyes were wide open. Young Kia looked him up and down. He had on a pair of Louis Vuitton briefs and matching bed slippers.

"Who is calling you like that?" she boldly asked.

"Probably your sister. And she's a year older than you so she might whip dat ass once she finds out you are over here with me."

"What? Please!" Kia said. "Ain't my fault niggas be wanting to jump ship when they see me. She better step her game up."

Rod laughed, then put some heat to the blunt that was resting on his nightstand. "Don't flatter yourself, ma. Star got you beat body, mind, and realness. Shorty got heart for days. What you got?"

"I am *more* than what your eyes can see. And obviously I'm something. Your dick hard already." Rodney looked down at himself and smiled before plucking ashes from his blunt.

"Stray pussy always excites me. Plus the fact that I'm basically fucking your whole family excites me. You were just the last of the Mohicans, baby girl." Rodney was coldhearted. Every word that left his mouth usually was below zero.

"You always got something to say. And Star is not the baddest chick in the world. I don't know why you act like that over her." Star was 15 and Kia, her older sister, was 16. They ran around without any guidance and no rules to govern their young lives. Men like Rodney ate them up and spit them back out, used and abused.

"She is not the baddest chick in the world, just the baddest in y'all family. I already fucked your mother. I fucked your aunt Gina *and* your grandmother. Now let me play with that thang. As long as I give 'em that good work, it's whatever," Rodney said with a smirk. He saw the disgusted look on Kia's face, and then burst into laughter.

Kia knew what was up with her aunt and mother. They were both fiends and prostitutes. Both dying from AIDS. But Kia knew better than to say something to Rodney about it. Instead, she decided to back out of what she had originally planned to do with him. She stood up.

"You fucked my grandmother?"

"Did I stutter?"

"I'm out of here, Rodney. That is going *too* far."

He reached out his hand and grabbed her arm. "Sit."

"I wanna go home."

"Don't use that little-girl voice now, baby girl. You're not going anywhere. You made your way into the lion's den, and I believe it's mating season now. We ain't 'bout to play your li'l fucking game."

"You're the one with the games, Rodney. You should have never opened your mouth about who all you fucked in my family. Then you gonna say the only reason you want me is basically to fulfill your little fantasy. Hell, no! You are *not* getting this tonight." She snatched her arm back and began buttoning up her shirt.

"You doing all this dressing up for nothing, shorty. Ain't no way you leaving out this den unfucked."

Kia suddenly became nervous. She looked toward the door. Rodney was wearing a satanic-looking grin on his face.

"So what you saying? You gon' rape me, Rodney?"

"I wouldn't call it rape . . . but something similar," he said taking another pull off the weed. Then he put it down and stood up over her. He dropped his briefs. Kia sucked her teeth and before Rodney continued with his demonic plan, his phone began vibrating. He looked at it, and then looked back at Kia.

"Rodney, I want to go home."

"Would you shut the fuck up?" he said angrily. Then he backhanded her. His phone vibrated again.

"But—"

"Shhh! Hello?" he answered the phone in a frustrated and aggravated tone. "What? Now? A'ight, I'll be right there." He hung up and looked at Kia sitting nervously on the bed.

"Get out! And your ass is lucky I got grown-bitch pussy waiting on me someplace else." Kia grabbed her shit and ran out of there as fast as she could.

Rodney was as mean as they come. But the soft side of him took over whenever he was around Von. Von was his world. In his own mind, he loved her very deeply. When Von was a young girl, he took her under his wing. His reputation in the street was that of a serious hustler. He kept his private sexcapades a secret. Von was only 14 when she came under his care. It was her fifteenth birthday, and he went all out for her. She had called him Uncle Rodney since he was 21, but he told her she didn't have to call him that anymore. He went from being an older brother figure, to getting up in her heart and panties.

He was the first person to ever introduce Von to a wild orgasm using his thunder tongue. As he drove to meet up with his boy, he reminisced on his first encounter with the love of his life.

"Come upstairs for a minute, Von." She left the party and headed upstairs with Rod. She trusted him like she did her brother. They were getting big money together back then, and Nasty vouched for him.

"Whassup?" she asked curiously. He patted the bed next to him.

"Have a seat. I wanted to give you a special gift." He reached behind the bed and gave her a small box. It was

wrapped in gold paper with a pink bow on top.

"You didn't have to. The party was nice enough." She opened the box, and there was a pair of diamond earrings shining so bright they almost blinded her.

"You like?"

"Oh my gosh. This is too much. Thank you. I don't know what to say."

"Let me put them in your ears." She swooped her long hair to one side, revealing her ear and a neck that were screaming out to be sucked. Rodney leaned in real close as he put her earring in. "You are a woman now."

"I'm far from a woman."

"But you carry yourself better than most of these bitches running around here that claim to be grown. I wish I had you on my arm." She slid away from him. "Relax, Von. You know I would never do anything to hurt you. I vowed to always protect you. Don't you know I'll protect you, baby?"

"Yeah, I know."

"So, let me protect you," he said to her softly. He was a master manipulator. Like a serpent, snakelike, he went for the bite. He licked her neckline and ended it with a kiss. Von's young innocence was being tested. He ran his fingers through hers and began kissing on her neck. She was young and vulnerable.

"Rodney, what are you doing?" she asked without

resisting.

"I'm going to please you, real quick."

"But I'm a virgin. I don't wanna have sex yet."

"And we won't." Rod had pinned her legs to her head and pounded her pussy with his tongue like oil would surge at any moment. She made sounds that even shocked her. Then he suddenly stopped.

"Wha-what're you doing?" she said in a breathy tone.

"Go back to the party. I don't people to start wondering where you are."

She pulled her panties up and made her way back to the party. But she was forever changed. She had never felt this way before, and her young body was curious and hungry for more.

After the party, Rod had licked her box all night long. But he was careful not to have sex with her. He wanted to reel her in and make her want him just as much as he wanted her. And it worked. After a few months of this, she was begging for him to have sex with her.

Once the word had surfaced that Rodney was packing a penis no bigger than that of an 8-year-old, he couldn't get women to sleep with him. So instead of looking for someone who would accept him for him, he stopped going after grown women and instead, started messing with young girls. He loved 'em around 14 or 15. They didn't know any better. And with Rodney's money, they all thought they had

16

hit the jackpot. He usually used 'em, and then threw the girls away like trash. But there was something about Von that he liked, and he wanted to keep her for himself.

His infected dick had been all over the city. He lurked at high schools and preyed on young girls like the villain he was. He was pathetic. Many girls were walking around sick just like Von. It was a horrible truth, and most had no idea.

He was on his way to pick up some dope, but got sidetracked. A young girl was crossing the street sucking on a lollipop. Rod rolled down his window. "Where you on your way to, shorty?" He couldn't help himself. Rodney was like a wild dog in heat.

CHAPTER 3

Nasty and Soulja were up at five in the morning, every day. But today, it was almost six, and they still hadn't started their workout. Nasty walked down to Soulja's cell, and Soulja looked at his watch. "You're late," he said.

"Man, come on so we can get this good workout in. I had to go handle a few things first. It's still early." Every morning, the two of them dressed in track Nikes, torn T-shirts, and mesh shorts, and they worked out for 2 hours. They did 1,000 push-ups, 500 burpies, and 2,000 sit-ups. Twenty minutes of shadow boxing, and then, finally, the torturous 5-mile run. At least, that's how Nasty felt. He hated running, but he knew he would never hear the end of it from Soulja if he bailed on it. So he made the agonizing run with the man he called his brother. This was their routine. By the time they came back inside, they were both sweating profusely.

"Damn, y'all are like robots," a voice said standing over them. It was an older cat, Mo Garrett. He had become a prison father to them.

"We gotta keep our shit solid. Never know when it's time for war," Nasty replied, still winded coming in from the run.

"A faithful man to his body is a man half-prepared for war," Mo Garrett said. He was always schooling them to something.

"What the hell does that mean?" Nasty asked.

"Simple. A lion is strong and heartless, but those same gifts could lead him into a trap. If you can't outthink your enemy, or at least be able to think on his level, you will always make an easy target."

"You always got some jewels to drop, Islamic Moor."

"And you should listen to the brother," Soulja added, now standing up, wiping his forehead with a rag. Both Soulja and Nasty were rock solid. Their bodies were so tight that a few female COs had to be disciplined for making inappropriate comments about them. Of course, the two men didn't mind, but the hating-ass men around them dropped a few dimes, saying that their exchanges were inappropriate.

The three men separated and showered, then they came back to eat in Nasty's cell. Mo Garrett was a professional microwave chef. He made them all a large pizza which they devoured like hungry beasts.

"What's wrong with you?" Soulja asked Nasty as they ate.

"Nothing. Why you ask?"

"Nicca, I know you better than you know yourself. You kept up with me the entire run, meaning you had extra energy to expel. Whattup?" Nasty sat back in his seat and folded his arms across his chest.

"It's Von. This is the second visit she's missed. That shit ain't like her." Before Soulja could respond, Mo Garrett did. He stroked the hair on his long beard and looked up at the young man he considered to be like a son.

"She is a young woman. This is what they do. She'll be back around eventually. I've seen it thousands of times over these past 22 years. Don't make more of it than what it is." Then he bit into his pizza.

"I can't catch her at home when I call. She's not answering my letters. It's just not like her. Something isn't right."

"You're acting paranoid. She's all right," Mo Garrett said calmly.

"Yeah, Mo is probably right. You know sis. She's probably got her head in them books."

"I hope y'all right."

"Hope? When have I ever told you a lie?" Mo asked.

"Never!"

"Glad you know it."

"And you know I love Von just as much. Plus, if something was wrong, Rodney would have got at you."

"Yeah, I guess. It's just that Von is all I got left. I just pray that nicca Rodney ain't putting her through no bullshit. You know how I feel about that relationship anyway. Nigga is too old for her."

"Yeah, I agree. But she grown now, so we gotta deal with it," Soulja reminded.

"That's true, but she wasn't grown when they started fucking around. She's my baby. Would you be okay with a nigga like Rodney fucking with I'sa?"

"Please don't talk about li'l I'sa and men. She's only 5. So it ain't something I've had to take the time to even think about."

"Listen, I'm sure that dude Rod is not stupid. Only a fool would stick his hand in a pot of boiling water. I wouldn't bet a wooden nickel on him doing her wrong. He'd be committing suicide. But then again, these cats out there today really believe they've got nine lives," Mo Garrett added.

"That's a good point, but I'ma just think positive about the situation because if I think otherwise too much, I'll end up doing something real crazy."

"We can't afford that. Now, fellas, it's lesson time. How are you two coming along with the business plans we've been working on?"

"So far so good. I got a list of the abandoned houses. And I've got somebody on top of getting the official taxes owed so we can buy them," Soulja said.

"Very good, son. And what about you, Nasty? How is your part coming?"

"I got a couple of dudes ready to do the construction work. I just haven't really been focused since I haven't seen my sister. But I *am* going to have it together."

Mo Garrett had explained to them the importance of true wealth. Baltimore had hundreds of abandoned row houses. With the money they were getting in prison, they planned to buy up a bunch of them, fix them up, and rent them at decent prices. They would be drug-free zones that come with their own hood security. They were also building a boxing gym for young boys and an etiquette school for young girls. They had big plans.

"Don't lose focus, Nasty. The one who has plans to go out and continue in the drug game has plans to return to prison—or make a permanent home in the ground. Any ideas for a name?"

"Yeah, I thought about it," Nasty said. "CHOICES. And it stands for Changing the Hearts of Innocent Children Enduring Strife."

Soulja dapped him. "That's dope right there, bruh!"

"Excellent," is all Mo Garrett said. "I'm going to temple . I'll see y'all later." He got up to leave. Just as Mo left, one of Nasty and Soulja's workers, Rocky, walked into the cell. He passed Soulja a half ounce of raw dope. Soulja examined it.

"This good work," Soulja said back.

"Yeah, the visit went good. Your girl said you need to call her. And she said to tell you I'sa beat up a li'l boy at school."

Soulja smiled, and then nodded. His daughter was just like him, and he loved her more than he loved himself. To keep the police confused, Soulja's girl didn't visit with him and bring work. She came to see Rocky and passed the shit to him. Sometimes Von would bring work too, but she had been missing in action lately. So Keva would make up the difference and come on visits to see Rocky. Then Rocky came back to the unit and brought the dope to Soulja and Nasty. They were running a small empire inside the penitentiary walls. On average, they were bringing in $5,000 to $7,000 a week selling dope. They had all kinds of customers. At first, they were just chilling, but when there was a drought a few months ago, it was their turn to take over. And they'd done an excellent job of running things.

But not everybody was feeling the two new CEOs on the block. There were a couple of cats that had been getting money in the prison before Nasty and Soulja started going hard. But they fell off. Nasty and Soulja could have got things popping a long time ago, but they were respectful to the older cats that had been down longer trying to eat. But there was a need that had to be filled, and when the opportunity presented itself, they opened up shop. And they did it with such precision, nobody else could set up shop. But that wasn't their fault. They let as many people eat as possible and ran a smooth operation.

It was important for Nasty to stay focused. He was the one with the least amount of time, unlike Soulja, who had a life sentence. So everything was riding on Nasty with CHOICES so that he could get out and make a difference. The drug game would end for them once Nasty got out. And Soulja could do his time in peace, knowing that his brother was living comfortably.

Nasty took it hard, knowing that his brother Soulja might not ever come home. He filed a few appeals, and they had all been denied so far. But Soulja wasn't called Soulja for no reason; he was just that—a soldier—and he would fight to the bitter end.

Nasty split up the work and put his workers on it. Today was collection day and also delivery day. The fiends who owed money would pay right away because they couldn't bear the idea of there being fresh dope within arm's reach and not being able to get high. They would call home and tell their mothers, brothers, daughters, cousins, wives, whomever they could get, to drop money to the spot so they could get their issue. It was an ugly yet beautiful reality. Survival of the fittest.

Nasty focused on his work to keep his mind off of his sister. They were so close that he could feel when something was wrong. He just knew it, even though he didn't have any facts. His intuition had never failed him. He loved his sister with all his heart. His arms were covered in tattoos. So was his chest and back. But the tattoo he loved the most was the tatt of Von and his mother Kay.

He wanted to come home one day and live in peace. He didn't want to have to go back to his old ways. After seeing his parents' dead bodies, death had become easy to hand out. Anybody got in his way, they would find themselves decaying not long after. Nasty was a very dangerous man. Almost all of his heart had hardened, minus the part that Von managed to keep soft. He just hoped that nothing was happening that would bring out the murderous side of him. He tried to shut down that part of himself, because once activated, there was no off button!

CHAPTER 4

"Girl, I would have sworn Moses to hell if anybody ever told me that Tony had eyes for anybody other me. But I got my bubble burst last night."

Paige and Von were out at their other close friend's house, Marla. The three of them were thick as thieves. Paige and Von had not yet told Marla about Von's sickness. They felt it was going to be too much for Marla to handle. However, that wasn't the issue at hand tonight. While Von was dealing with her health, Paige was dealing with problems in her relationship. She'd been with Tony for years. Ever since they were young. They were the perfect couple . . . until rumors started surfacing about Tony doing things he shouldn't with another woman. Paige didn't want to believe that the father of her child and love of her life would do her wrong. But the evidence was staring her in the face.

"What are you talking about, Paige?" Marla asked.

"Yes, please enlighten us," Von added.

"You think Tony is cheating on you?" Marla inquired.

"I don't *think* he is. I *know* it!"

"Girl, shut up! No! Not the Mr. Wannabe-Perfect, preaching-ass nigga, Tony. Let me find out he got caught slippin'," Marla said.

"Well, let me tell y'all. I went home after leaving Von's house last night. Tony wasn't home. I started washing clothes, and I found some chick named Sharise's number in his pocket."

"Girl, that's it? That might not even mean nothing," Von said.

"Hold up, it gets better. So you know Tony's little brother sounds just like him, even though he's only 14. So I went to Tony's mother's house and had his little brother call the girl number with the phone on speaker. I had to pay him $100 to do it."

"Girl, you ain't shit," Marla said laughing.

Von just shook her head. "Okay, so what happened?"

"So the girl answers and his li'l brother says, 'Yo, baby, this Tony. What you doing?' girl in his best Tony voice."

"This shit is unreal. Wait . . . This is too good," Marla said unable to hold her laughter. Von was not laughing. The thought of another possibly unfaithful man did not amuse her.

"Marla, our girl is hurting, and you acting like you watching Jerry Springer or soap operas."

"Okay, okay. My bad. I'm sorry. What happened?" she

asked, trying to be serious.

"So the chick wants to know who is playing on the phone. I took that as a good sign. I was about to hang up until someone else grabbed the phone. It was Tony."

"What?" Marla and Von said in unison.

"Yup! That muthafucka wanted to know who was calling his house."

"*His house?*" they said in unison again.

"Yes, girl. So I said, 'What the hell do you mean your house, Tony? Bitch, when you asked me to marry your big dumb ass you was serious. Now you claiming the next bitch house? I thought you lived over here with me and your daughter.'"

"Hold up a minute, baby!" Tony said with fear in his voice.

"No, don't tell me to hold up. You're a fucking dog. A liar. A snake. I don't want shit to do with you, Tony. I mean it, nigga. And this cheap-ass engagement ring you bought me will be in the same pocket I found this number in—with the rest of your shit on the curb."

"Oh no! Paige, that's fucked up," Marla said.

"I was screaming so loud at him that I woke up the baby. But that is not the icing on the cake. In the background, Sharise starts screaming at Tony. She tells him to get dressed and pack his shit and get the fuck out now! He then yells to her to shut the fuck up. And that this is all a misunderstanding. He started saying that it's not like that, and he is not fucking with her on no sexual shit. But his spot had already been blown up. I just couldn't believe it."

"So you mean to tell me he was trying to explain shit to her too?" Von asked.

"Yes, I heard it with my own ears. The two of them were arguing back-and-forth. There was a lot of screaming. I couldn't make out everything. Then the bitch picks up the phone and tells me that he lied to both of us, and that she told him to leave. So I told her if he ain't packed up and out of her house in 10 minutes, to call me back, and we can beat his ass together. She agreed and told me don't lose no sleep over his bum ass."

"Paige, this is too much. I can't believe this shit," Von said.

"You sure you don't wanna go fuck him *and* this bitch up? You think she really put him out?" Marla questioned.

"Man, I don't know. I don't know. It's all bad." Paige burst into tears. Marla and Von ran to her side to comfort her.

"I can't front, I would have never thought Tony would do anything like this. I'm sorry, Paige," Marla said.

"These men ain't shit," Von said.

"Sure ain't. And, Paige, you need to get tested because these men be throwing around raw dick like it's not an epidemic in the city. You lucky he didn't bring home no

AIDS or nothing. You better get you and your baby tested just to be sure, even though it's probably nothing," Marla said, shaking her head.

The room became eerily silent. Marla had no idea about Von's illness. Von put her head down. She had gotten so caught up in the matter at hand that she pushed her own situation to the back of her mind for a moment. And now it was front and center. There was nothing selfish about Von. This was Paige's crisis, so she focused on that.

"So, hold up . . . Did he ever come back over here?" Von asked.

"No. I called his phone and didn't get an answer. So I called the chick Sharise's phone back, and she answered. Tony was still there. And you know what the bitch said?"

"I don't know if I can take it. What did she say?" Marla asked.

"She told me don't call back there. And to leave her and Tony alone. If I called back, she would call the police and tell them I've been harassing them."

"Oh, hell, no! That bitch need her ass royally stomped on," Von said.

"Let's go over there right now, Paige."

"Yes, we need to give that bitch one of our seasonal beat downs that we used to be known for." Von had tears running down her face for her girl. Marla was too mad to cry.

"It's all good. I'll be okay. If that's where he wants to be, let him stay," Paige said. "I got a little girl to think about."

"I just can't believe this," Von said. "You need to cut his ass all the way off!" She knew her girl was hurting. Tony and Paige had been together for 8 years. Since they were just 12 years old.

"I think we need to just go out there and do these niggas the same way they've been doing us. Switch 'em up like tampons. Trade 'em in for a new model every year like a leased car. Play with their feelings and let them see how it feels," Marla said.

"Hell, no, Marla. That wouldn't do us no good. That's nasty. All it would do is get y'all sick with HIV or some shit like how Rodney did me."

"Hold up! What did you say?" Marla asked.

"Yes, I might as well put it out there to you. I am HIV-positive. Rodney gave it to me."

Marla fell back onto the couch and covered her mouth. It was as if her ears were playing a horrible trick on her.

"I am 18 years old—with HIV."

Von was the youngest of the three, so immediately, Marla was traumatized. Marla's world was rattled beyond belief. Her two closest friends—her sisters—were going through hell. She almost felt guilty for not having a problem of equal magnitude. She hoped this was a bad dream. Maybe she'd wake up tomorrow, and none of this would have happened. Von wouldn't be sick, and Paige's family would be back intact. But she pinched herself and quickly realized this was very real. Then she thought maybe it was a bad joke. But neither of them would play with such foul information. Marla began crying hysterically. She started thinking about Von being dead. The thought brought on immediate nausea.

Von walked over to Marla and embraced her. She was calm. "Don't cry, Marla. I'm gonna be all right. God's got me. I decided last night not to cry over what's done. I'm just gonna accept the plan that has been laid out for me and deal with it. I'm going to give my life to God."

"Girl, if God was real, he wouldn't let this shit happen to you. You don't deserve this. And I don't wanna hear shit 'bout God!" Marla screamed. Both of her girls had been hit with gut punches. They weren't in the streets running wild. They were in school, they worked, they were about their business. And now, just like that, their lives were in shambles.

"Shh! You're gonna wake the baby up," Paige said. "She's probably looking for her father. He always puts her to sleep." The three women were going through it.

"Von, what are going to do?" Marla asked as snot and tears ran down her face.

"There is nothing we can do. Well, there is nothing *I* can do, but Paige can. She can get as far away from Tony as possible."

"And what about Rod? What does *he* have to say about this?" Marla asked.

"I don't think he even knows. I fucked with that dog-ass nigga, and now his ass gonna follow me to my grave. I could see him dead right now, but I ain't got the heart to kill nobody."

"This is too much. All at once, the two people I would literally die for are going through hell. This is a cruel-ass world," Marla said sadly.

"Yes, it is. But we just gotta pull our shit together," Von said. Marla and Paige both sucked strength from Von. If she could be so strong, so could they.

"I have an idea," Marla said. "As of tomorrow, the three of us will look for a three-bedroom town house and move in together. This way, we can all support and help each other with bills and whatever else this world throws at us."

"Cool. Then Tony and Rodney won't know where to find us," Paige added.

"I'm with it. But I have one requirement, y'all. I don't care what happens, but my brother can never *ever* know I'm infected. Please! Promise me!"

"I don't know about that, Von. That is your brother, and he thinks he's your father. He needs to know," Marla said.

"Hell, no! He already has enough on his plate. He doesn't need to know that Rodney basically condemned the one person he has left. Hell, no. Promise me! Right here—right now!"

"Okay!" Marla said.

"I promise," Paige said.

"Oh, and one more thing. I was supposed to take some dope up to the prison for Nasty. I usually pass him the work by kissing him, but I don't wanna kiss and pass no work through my mouth to my brother, knowing I'm infected. I don't feel comfortable. So would you take it up there for me, Marla?" Von asked.

"Anything for you. Plus, I don't mind kissing Nasty's fine ass. He's always wanted me and never made a move. But I might kiss him for real tomorrow."

"Your ass is crazy, girl. That's on you if you wanna start messing with my crazy-ass brother. I know he is going to ask you why I didn't come. Just tell him I've been studying in school real hard."

"I got you, girl." The three of them gave each other a big hug, and they all shared a laugh.

That night, an even deeper bond was formed among the three young women. They were going to ride the wave of the storm and try their best to dance in the rain.

CHAPTER 5

Nasty whistled to the officer walking the tier. No words needed to be spoken; he knew what Nasty wanted. He nodded and came back with a towel roll and passed it to him. Nasty opened it and went to the corner of his room to use what was inside. A cell phone. He immediately called his boy, Moon. He needed to know what the hell was going on and how he had lost contact with his sister.

"I don't know what the fuck is going on with Von, but you're supposed to be on top of that shit, Moon. We already discussed this. My hands are tied behind my back while I'm in the joint, dawg. So you being my man are supposed to easy my troubles," Nasty said, frustrated as hell. He called his boy Moon from a contraband cell phone. He paid an officer for it, and the officer kept it most times so he wouldn't get caught with it. He was smart; he only used it sometimes, like when he needed to talk business. Most people got caught because they overdid it.

"Yo, I went past the crib, and she wasn't there. As a matter of fact, it looked abandoned."

"What?"

"I been calling the crib. She hasn't been answering the phone or her cell phone. I keep getting voice mail, so *you* tell me what *you* want me to do," Moon said. Nasty kept Moon on a payroll to handle things in the street for him and to keep an eye on Von. But he wasn't doing a good enough job the way Nasty saw it.

"What do *I* want *you* to do? Nigga, buy some fucking well-bred bloodhounds and have them track her ass down," Nasty said. He was joking, but his voice evoked so much fear, that Moon didn't know whether to laugh or start googling the Internet looking for dogs for real.

"Well, that would be nice, but this ain't the Westerns or slavery time, bruh." Awhile back, Nasty had asked Moon to put a tracker on Von's car but quickly opted out once he remembered that Rodney usually had the car swept for bugs since he was so deep in the drug game. He'd find it and think the feds did it.

"Look, I just need to know my little sister is okay. I need you to prioritize getting in touch with her."

"I got you. Just give me until the end of the day. I'll find her. She can't be far."

"I'm worried about her. Ever since her ass turned 18,

she's been on some bullshit. I been keeping money in her pocket and paying her bills and shit, 'cause I don't want no nigga holding nothing over her head, feel me? And now her li'l ass has gone AWOL on me."

"Ain't nothing about Von's ass little," Moon said, teasing his man.

"Fuck you just say?" Nasty asked.

"You know I'm just messing with you. But you gonna have to accept the fact that Von grown now. She not running on the block with her friends throwing water balloons at us no more. She a woman. With her own life. You gon' drive yourself crazy."

"Don't worry about me. Just do what I asked."

"I'm on it."

"And keep your ears to the street. If anything ain't right with my sister, I give you permission to do what's necessary."

"I got you."

"Never will I forget you, Moon. You been holding me down. We come from the same sandbox, my dude, but you should know that if I feel in any way that you cannot handle the jobs I have lined up for you, or you're not mentally ready to take on the tasks I ask, I *will* replace you and not fuck with you," Nasty warned.

"And what is my first task?"

"You let me know when you're ready to say good-bye

to that sweet girl called the game, and I'll let you know. That means side hustling and all."

"Damn, you asking me to throw away everything I know. You must have a real good task."

"It is. But you are welcome to stay in the game, keep selling dope forever. You can even spend $360 a month for the rest of your life once you get that fed time. And I'll be sure to keep it on your books. You can count on that," Nasty said sarcastically.

"That's a foul way for me to end it, man, but I feel you."

"I need you to do more than feel me. We making that transition, and I want you on the team." A lot of dudes in their neighborhood were talented businessmen. It's just that the business they were running was illegal. The transition was scary because it was foreign to them.

"I'ma make it happen. I'm with you about going legit, and I'll let you know when. But it's not today and not tomorrow. I got a 150-pound Rottweiler to feed and a bunch of greedy kids at the crib. I can't transition yet. But I'ma start getting my mind right."

"Good. So tell me this, who is making the most noise in the streets right now?" Nasty asked.

"Your sister's boyfriend is doing his thing. He called himself buying out the entire bar last week at Club Trill."

"Oh yeah?"

"Yeah, the nicca believe in stuntin', and he keep a

couple'a trigger-happy young cats with him at all times."

"I guess he feel like that's enough to save his life if a nigga wanna claim his head, huh?" Nasty presumed.

"Well, if he know like I know, when that AK go, it's the end of the show," Moon said.

"You better believe it!"

"Man, Nasty, you should have seen this clown. He had the nerve to approach me, with his six-shooters beside him and ask me if I would join his team."

"You lying dog," Nasty said unable to hold his laughter.

"I never knew he was on some Frank shit from *Scarface*. Actually, he talked like was the last Don. He was posing with his arms folded across his crotch and everything." Nasty had folded over in laughter. "Hold up, Nasty, it's even better. He tells me that him and his brother Lucky been doing some serious thinking. And he wants to put his family's safety first. He said my name came up at the top of the list to be their hired gunman. The shit was so funny, because this nigga was talking like he was a Mob boss, with the accent and everything."

"This shit sounds unbelievable," Nasty said, almost unable to talk. Inside, he was fuming because he realized even more that his sister was with a clown. A real live joker. "I hope you checked that muthafucka."

"You know I did. I said, 'Listen here, Don Corleone, I never knew you were Italian; otherwise, I would've been called a meeting with your ass. You chose the wrong man to offer a fuck boy job to. I been a boss in these streets. Frankly, I could care less about you or your brother Lucky. My affairs are with Von. That's it. And if I had any say, you wouldn't even be fucking with her at all. I don't respect cats that kill a good man to get to the top, get all his soldiers locked up, and then resurface, claiming to be the King of the Streets. Ky was a real G. You did him dirty, and I don't respect you. So thank you for the offer, but you can take yo' ass back to Italy!'"

"You handled that shit just right." Nasty's laughter had long been gone. He started thinking about other good cats that had mysteriously "gone missing," and now it made sense. It was probably Rodney knocking people off so he could run the show.

"See, Nasty, when you get home, your takeover will be easy. Ol' boy could get his teeth stomped out, and I'll be right there beside you to collect 'em."

"Nah, you must've missed our whole conversation earlier. Me and Soulja are out of the game. We're done. I'm serious about going legit. I'm not even trying to pick them guns back up."

"Nasty, you without guns is like the sun without rays. Your name in itself came from you being so nasty with them weapons."

"Yeah, well, I'm not trying to go there. Of course, I will kill for my loved ones. That goes without question, but I am not going to be that reckless, lost, young cat I used to be. Them days are over. The street hustle is a cash business. So everybody is after what you got. Once we go legit, money will be in banks and shit. We won't have to stash half a mill in the basement, another mill in the attic, another mill buried in the backyard. There will be no need for all that gunplay. It's a better life."

"All right, fam, I hear you talking. I got you. I'm on the hunt for Von, and I'll get at you with an update as soon as possible."

Nasty felt like his man wasn't getting it. But that was okay. He could show him better than just tell him.

"Peace, Moon, and protect ya neck!"

"One, love."

Nasty hung up the phone, and then whistled for the CO. He slid him the phone and some dope. That was the way things worked. It was a dog-eat-dog world in the United States penitentiary. Everybody needed to eat, and everybody tried to survive. His mind was all over the place. He knew that Rod was not the best man in the world for his sister, but he had to make a fast decision when he got locked up to protect her. Now he was regretful. He didn't want her with him, but he also knew how much she loved him, and he didn't want her in any pain at all.

He could kill Rodney, but all that would do is grieve Von, and he couldn't have that. She'd been through enough pain. He didn't want to add to it. All in all, the most important thing to him was getting out and going legit. That is all that mattered. Then he could get Von himself, and find a suitable man for her.

CHAPTER 6

The girls found a town house and went out to celebrate. When they put their minds to something, it usually happened. They were at Club Trill, trying their best to enjoy life, even though they all felt like their lives were falling apart.

"Paige, damn, girl! That ass sitting up like you Serena Williams or something. I knew you was stuffed but not like a turkey," Mad-Dog said. He stood six foot three and towered over Paige. He was cut up, with a swollen chest and arms that looked like he just finished benching a house. His chain had no piece drooping from it. He rocked one long platinum chain with no less than 60 pea-sized diamonds hanging from his neck. His complexion was perfect. His skin looked like it had been dipped in milk chocolate. Paige had a thing for shoes, so when she peeped the Hershey-colored alligator Giuseppe sneakers, she smiled.

While Rodney had become a big deal in East Baltimore, everybody knew that Mad-Dog was moving major weight all over Maryland and Virginia. He wasn't cocky with it. He was smooth and exuded the demeanor of a true boss. He'd been looking at Paige for years, but she had made it clear she was in a relationship, so nobody came at her. But tonight, her energy was very different. Mad-Dog looked Paige up and down, and he might as well have had his tongue hanging out of his mouth. Nobody had seen Paige dressed like this in a long time.

"I see you are liking what you see," Von said to Mad-Dog. "She look good, don't she?"

"Looking good is an understatement," he replied.

"That's because this is the first time in a long time Paige has been free to play," Von said, trying to encourage Mad-Dog to go after her girl.

"Why don't you and your girls come sit up in VIP with me and da' homies. Unless your boy Tony would have an issue with that. I'm not trying to disrespect nobody," he said.

"Tony? Please. Tony's ass went out with last week's trash."

Marla and Von giggled silently with each other. Paige had a couple of drinks so she was saying what was really on her mind.

"I just seen that cat Tony strolling through not too long ago. So don't get yourself caught up," Mad-Dog warned.

"Nah, we're good," Paige insisted. "Let's go sit. My feet

hurt," she said. They walked over to VIP and sat down. Paige threw her legs over Mad-Dog's lap and started laughing at nothing in particular. Mad-Dog peeped her game, but he let her play. He thought it was cute. Von and Marla sat in the booth as well and Mad-Dog began introducing them to his boys.

"This is Sconey, Charlie, and Marvin. All my mans from up McCabe," Mad-Dog said. The men were all respectful and spoke kindly to the ladies. Sconey had his eye on Von, and Mad-Dog peeped it. "You sit tight, young lady. I'm hip to who you are." She assumed he was referring to the fact that she was Rodney's girl, but he didn't even acknowledge that. "You're my man Nasty's li'l sister. That's one of the realest that ever done it, and I got mad respect for him. Which means she's off-limits." Then he looked at Marla. "And you, you used to hang around Soulja a lot. I don't know what that status is, but for now, your ass is off-limits too." Marla sucked her teeth.

"Damn, what, you keeping tabs on my girls?" Paige said.

"And my brother knows I am grown. So, Sconey, you are free to buy me a drink if you want."

Sconey smiled, then spoke. "Hell, naw. What you trying to do, baby girl, start a war? Everybody knows you fuck with Rodney, and he got that ass on lock."

"I don't mess with Rodney anymore," Von said. "But if you're scared, I understand." Mad-Dog and Sconey got a real kick out of that.

"Yeah, I'm so scared, I might let you post up with me for the rest of the night. Then you could ride shotgun in my Maserati later. How's that?" Sconey got up out of his seat and switched with Charlie so he could sit next to Von.

"Now, that's better," Von said.

Mad-Dog just shook his head and laughed. The waitress came over to the table, and Mad-Dog ordered 10 bottles of Ace of Spades and three bottles of Cîroc. He also got what looked like 100 chicken wings.

Paige's legs were slipping from his lap, so he grabbed them and put them back in place. His touch was respectful. He wasn't going to overstep his boundaries.

"So let me ask you a question, Paige. How come years of love and loyalty has gone out the window?" Mad-Dog asked out of curiosity. It really didn't matter, but he just wanted confirmation that it was really over between her and Tony. He knew that couples argued and sometimes did things out of anger.

"Well, let's just say he chose someone other than me." There was a sadness in her voice that let Mad-Dog know that shit was serious.

"Word? I don't see how that's possible. You're perfect from what I can see."

"Not to him, obviously," she said.

"Some men get tired of the same scenery and go out

looking for a new show. But they soon find out the new show is a dud. He'll be back."

"I don't want him back. But trust me, he is *definitely* missing the best thing he ever had."

"I can only imagine."

"Play your cards right and you won't have to imagine," she said flirtatiously. Just then, she spotted Tony. She instinctively moved her legs, but then thought better of it and pretended like she was getting comfortable. Then she wrapped her arms around Mad-Dog. He knew what was up, but continued to let her play.

Tony and Paige locked eyes. And instantly, hot lava ran through his veins. Paige was testing him, and he was about to let it be known that this shit was *not* okay. Paige smirked at the look of insanity on Tony's face. She smiled and turned her attention back to Mad-Dog. It was her first time hanging out with a drug dealer and real thug. So his swag was setting her wick on fire.

Tony was not a hustler by any means. He was what the hood would have called a square. But Tony had heart. He'd let his gun off a few times before over her. Some dudes tested him because he wasn't in the streets, thinking he was soft. But they quickly learned that he would do whatever over Paige. He had a job and worked a nine to five. He took care of his family, which consisted of Paige and their daughter.

He wasn't a broke dude, but he didn't have a whole lot

of money. That's why the ring he bought her was smaller than he wanted it to be. He paid cash and bought what he could afford. Paige didn't care about his status. She was happy to be engaged to the love of her life. She was with a man who was loyal and loving. But after seeing the jewels on Mad-Dog's neck and arms, and absorbing the boss-ass energy coming off of him, she felt like she deserved a little more.

Tony was indecisive about approaching Paige. He wasn't scared of Mad-Dog by any means, but he was scared of getting embarrassed by Paige and having his ego stomped on like a welcome mat after a snowy day. Mad-Dog checked the time on his Audemars Piguet.

"Paige, I know you see this psychotic-looking bastard staring over here like he wanna bite your head off," Marla said in a whisper. When Paige looked up, Tony had his arm stretched in front of him using his index finger, signaling for her to come over.

"You better go see what Slim want 'fore you get it, ma. Homeboy looking like the Texas Strangler right now," Mad-Dog joked.

"Whatever, Maddie," Paige said, brushing him off.

"Oh, so you calling me li'l nicknames now?" he said.

They shared a laugh, and this infuriated Tony. *This bitch must be out of her rabbit-ass mind*, Tony thought to himself. She ignored his request to come to him. She continued sitting all up on Mad-Dog. Rage had taken over

Tony's normal thought processes. He angrily approached VIP, and the bodyguards stepped in front of him.

"Let him up," Mad-Dog instructed. They moved out of the way.

"Mad-Dog, whattup?" Tony asked.

"Ain't shit, just doing what I do. What's been good with you, though?"

"Just trying to hold my temper together so I don't accidently snap Paige's neck."

Sconey and Charlie busted out laughing, fueling Tony's anger. But he tried to hold it together. Paige had turned her back to him. She decided to let her girls handle him. Von wanted to flip on Tony for threatening her girl like that. He had no right after what he did.

"Why don't you go somewhere, Tony," Marla said, with a screwed up expression on her face.

"Yeah. You're worried about the wrong female. You need to go find your bat. I think I saw her flying around here earlier," Von added.

"You couldn't even go get a bird bitch; you got a bat. Which really is just a rat with wings!"

Mad-Dog tried his best not to laugh. He felt Tony's pain.

"Forget y'all." He turned his attention to Paige. "Baby, I need to talk to you. We got years in. We have a daughter."

"She not trying to hear you, Tony. Leave it alone. She

went from a broke joke to a paid, made man. There is nothing you can do for her. Go back to Sharise or whatever that bitch name is. Bye!"

Tony was two seconds short of peeling off his own skin. "Paige!" he yelled.

Her response was to stroke the top of Mad-Dog's head, acting like Tony wasn't standing right there. He couldn't control himself and lunged for her. But Sconey stood in front him.

"Watch it. She's with us now." Sconey tapped his waist. Tony raised his hands showing that he wasn't trying to have that type of problem at the moment.

"Yo, Mad-Dog, my beef ain't with you, Slim, but I'm telling you now, Paige, if you try to keep my daughter away from me or have her around any other cat, I'ma hang your ass from the top of that telephone pole in front of the house. I swear to God on that one, baby." Paige paid him no attention.

"Party's over. This ain't the place for all these threats," Sconey said.

"Sconey, I'ma respect game where games is played. Just respect mine when I lay it down." Tony winked his eye at Paige, and then turned and walked away. It took about 15 minutes for the stench of his anger to fade away and everybody could go back to chilling. Paige was feeling tipsy, so she hadn't absorbed the full blow of Tony's fury.

It was three in the morning when everybody headed to the parking lot. Mad-Dog made sure the ladies were escorted to their car. His crew had the place looking like some top NBA players had parked out front. Mad-Dog's li'l men had been holding fort like the Secret Service out front. All three of their cars were bulletproof, and all of his men were holding AR-15 handguns.

"So, Maddie, you keep this kind of protection everywhere you go?" Paige asked.

"Nah, this only for nightclubs, shorty. It's always somebody laying in the cut waiting to catch a nicca slippin'. So if that target is me, they gets no chance. Plus, I can hold my own."

"Maybe you can hold me," Paige said stumbling. Mad-Dog caught her by her elbow and stood her up straight. He was glad she wasn't driving and walked her to the backseat of Von's 5 Series BMW.

"Nah, I'm good. That's not happening."

"So you're not feeling me?" she asked leaning up against the car and pulling Maddie close to her.

"I'm not saying that. First, I don't trust you. And second, I don't take advantage of vulnerable women. If something happens between us, it will be because it was supposed to. Not like this. Have a good night, baby." He turned and walked over to his Bentley Bentayga truck.

"Damn!" Paige, Marla, and Von said in unison. They watched him drive off.

"Whelp, Tony can kiss his old life good-bye," Marla said.

They recognized that not only was Mad-Dog a real G, but he was the perfect gentleman as well. Shit was about to change.

CHAPTER 7

Nasty was sitting at the table in his cell composing a letter to his sister when Soulja walked into his room.

"Have you heard from our li'l sis yet?" Soulja asked.

"Nah. That shit got me stressed. I don't know what the hell is—" their conversation was interrupted by a CO screaming out to Nasty that he had a visit. He was already dressed, because he had gone to the barbershop earlier and got a fresh cut just in case Von decided to show up and explain her disappearing acts. Besides, there were a bunch of young and vulnerable female COs that just got hired the other day. They were always choosing, and Nasty was always on the hunt for new employees to put on his payroll. So he kept his shit fresh and made it easily known that he was penitentiary ballin'. The females were the easiest to recruit. Immediately, they could see that Nasty and Soulja were getting money, usually more than the man they had in the streets or at home was making. It didn't take much to turn one bad.

"Take this," Soulja said sliding Nasty $9,000 in cash.

"Whoever it is down there, give them this bread and tell 'em to drop it off to my daughter. I'sa is about to start second grade soon, and I want my baby girl to learn the art of flossin' early."

Nasty shook his head and laughed. "I got you." He left and headed toward the visiting room. He raised his arms out to the side of him so the guard could pat him down. The correction officer did a lousy job, because he didn't check Nasty's socks where he had the money stashed. If he would have gotten caught, he would have just given the guard a couple hundred to make sure he stayed quiet. Not even the guards wanted beef with him or Soulja. Nobody was exempt from their wrath—and everybody knew it.

When Nasty walked into the visiting room, his smile lit up the place. Finally. Von! He exhaled. Sitting next to her was fine-ass Marla. Von wasn't originally going to come along, but once she heard how Nasty had the entire streets looking for her, she decided to show up. She didn't want to come alone, though, so she took Marla for support. Marla stood up and reached out to him.

Nasty embraced her. Marla was sexy, but he had more pressing matters at hand . . . like what the hell was going on with his sister? But Marla was not backing down. She reached out and pulled him in close. Her lips smacked against his, and she kissed him wildly. Nasty realized that she had something in her mouth. So he played the tongue swirling game with her until she passed him the small package. But she continued to kiss him even after the exchange was made. It felt passionate. He didn't expect that and immediately caught a hard-on. He hadn't kissed a woman like that in a long time. Years actually.

He coughed a few times afterward, and just like that, the work was out of his mouth and in his hands. In a few minutes, he planned to hide it in his socks. Usually he would have had to put it behind his nut sack, but the guard on duty was cool. So he didn't have to go to extremes.

"Hey, brother!" Von said. She stood up and hugged him. And he wasn't trying to notice, but he did. His sister was thicker than usual. He didn't like the fact that she was wearing tight leggings, and her ass was poking out.

"Don't 'hey, brother' me. And why the hell are you dressed like that? You need to cover up." Von looked down at herself and not one inch of flesh was showing. She was completely covered. But there wasn't much she could do about her shape. Von had gotten thick and people were always commenting about it. Her brother was always extra worrying about someone bothering her. She ignored him. He'd been like that ever since she was a little girl.

"So are you okay, bro?" she asked, trying to lighten the mood.

"No—I'm not. Where da fuck you been? I been going crazy up in here looking for you."

"I'm sorry, bro. I been so crazy with school. You know I'm going to the community college."

Marla, sensing Nasty was about to hit Von with 21 questions, chimed in. "You look good, Nasty. And you smell good as hell too."

"What you thought, I was gonna be looking like trash?"

"Not at all. I'm just still attracted to your handsome ass." Marla could see his physique through his clothing. She knew he was looking more than right.

"Nasty, I'm sorry about worrying you. I really am. Everything is okay with me."

"It's okay, baby girl. I just needed to know you were good."

"It won't happen again. The only time you won't hear from me from now on is if I'm not breathing."

"Well, I guess nobody will be hearing from either one of us if that was ever the case. Because you're the only reason I have to live. So we'd be kicking it in heaven."

"The two of y'all are crazy," Marla interrupted. Their closeness is what attracted Marla to him. She knew that if this is the way Nasty loved his sister, that if he had a woman, he'd love her more than she could even fathom. She was also very concerned. Von was the only blood family Nasty had left, and her medical situation would devastate him, possibly beyond repair. She thought that maybe she could give him another reason to live. Maybe they could make a life together once Nasty got out.

"Here, Von, take this money." He passed her the money

out of his socks. "Make sure that this gets to Keva and tell her it's for I'sa."

"Got you. How is Soulja doing, and how old is she now anyway?"

"I'sa is 5. Looking just like Soulja. He's good." Nasty really wanted to kick it with his sister, but Marla's beautiful body and face were distracting him. And knowing his little sister, she did that shit on purpose to keep her ass from getting screamed on. He had to laugh to himself at her cleverness.

"I'm going to the bathroom, I'll be right back," Von said, winking at Marla.

"So listen, I'm gonna get straight to the point. It's gonna be me doing the rest of this bid with you."

"Nah, I'm good. Trust me, baby, I'm not the one you want," he said.

"Yes, you are," she said punching him in the arm playfully. "Damn. Your shit is rock solid." He flexed and gave her the side eye.

"Why are you playing, Nasty? You been feeling me for years, and now that I'm with it, you acting like you don't want it. Men get on my nerves."

Nasty laughed at her little attitude. "Listen, seriously, a lot comes along with fucking with me. I'm not your average dude. I'm just chilling right now."

Marla was insulted. "Okay, well, I ain't no average

chick," is all she said. There was awkward silence between them.

"You mad now?"

"Nah, I'm good."

"It's not like that, Marla. But for real, it's a lot asking a female to ride this bid out with me. Don't get me wrong, I'm feeling you. That probably won't ever change. But I'm on something different. I need a woman that is going to take care of home and support my dreams."

"Hold up, support *your* dreams? What if she has dreams of her own?"

"Well, if they're good dreams and something on point, then that's even better, and I'll support in the same regard."

"You always gotta be so difficult."

"Life is difficult."

"No, Nasty, we make life difficult based on our choices. The only thing life gives us is the right to die. That's it," she said.

"Marly Marl droppin' jewels," he said smiling at her. "That was an actually very intelligent statement." Seeing Nasty smile was a gift in and of itself, because it wasn't something he did often. "We'll see where it goes from here, okay?"

"All right. I'm good with that," she said leaning over and kissing him on the cheek. She wanted to devour him, but she held it together. Von came out of the bathroom and sat back down.

"So, bro . . . Paige and Tony are not together anymore."

"Word? Tone and Paige? Why? After all these years and a baby?"

"It was Tony's dumb ass. He started fucking with some other chick. She found the girl's number in Tony's pocket and called. Tony was there with the girl, asking who was calling 'his' house."

"Damn. That nicca got caught slippin' real hard."

"Well, she was kicking it with Mad-Dog right in front of Tony. That's what his ass gets."

"Yeah, all that sounds good until Tony is holding a loaded .45 to her temple, ready to take her, the baby, and himself out. Y'all play too much."

Marla looked at him like he was crazy. Note taken. She knew never to play with his feelings.

"Well, I hope they don't get back together because cheating-ass men have no reason to live in my book."

"Let me ask y'all this. And I'm serious. Did Tony put his hands on Paige? You know Paige is family."

"Nah, brother. He tried to go after her, but Sconey stepped in the way. And Sconey and Mad-Dog spoke very highly of you."

"*That's* whassup. I'm just happy that he didn't put his hands on her. I know he was mad and all, but you know how I feel about that."

"He calmed down after that," Marla explained.

"So li'l sis . . . You've been awfully quiet. What's up with you and Rodney?" Her heart started beating extra hard in her chest.

"I'm gonna just be honest with you, bro. I'm done with him. He ain't no better than Tony. He out there messing with other girls while I'm at home playing housewife."

"I heard Rodney getting money right now. He just feeling himself. Money makes people cocky and wanna stretch their legs. They wanna enjoy the luxuries of getting paid."

"What?" Von said, shocked. She just knew that Nasty would be ready to put a hit out on Rodney for cheating on her. She was not liking his response.

"Von, I tried to school you when you were younger about fucking with a nigga in the drug game. This is what they do. Most men prefer pussy over gold."

"Nasty, I don't care. That doesn't give him the right to run around sleeping with chicks behind my back."

"I'm not saying it's okay, Von, but I told you what it was."

Von was pissed. Marla stayed out of it.

"You are saying it's okay. But it don't matter, I already moved out. I'm living with Marla and Paige. We got a town house together."

"Von, that dude made a way for you after I went to

prison. That's the only thing I respect about his fake ass. He put a lot of time and money into you, and if you think he is gonna sit back and watch you just walk away, then you really are just a baby."

"You know what? I don't need to hear this bullshit from you or anybody else. You so calm and smooth now, huh? Well, guess what? Tell that shit to some other bitch that they need to accept their cheating-ass man just because he sells drugs." She had never cursed at him before. He looked at her as if she was high.

"You been smoking or something, Von?"

"I should be asking *you* that. *You* are supposed to protect *me*. I can't believe you're okay with him cheating on me."

"I'm not okay with it, but I have always told you the real about life since you were 9. If you want me to start telling you some unrealistic bullshit, I can. But this is the raw. Men in the street do street shit. And fucking with a bunch of bitches is one of them. That's just the truth. This dude has given you everything, so y'all need to work it out."

"Yeah, he gave me everything. He even gave me—"

"Gave you what? A temporary broken heart? It'll be okay."

She wanted to say he gave me HIV, but she held her tongue.

"It won't be okay. I never thought I'd see the day my own brother would get soft. Damn, Rodney got everybody shook these days. I'll find someone to hold me down, though." Those words stung him. He knew she was upset, but that didn't make it hurt any less. He'd protected her all his life, with everything from his He-Man sword, to his Mac 10.

"Yo, CO, I'm ready to go back to my unit."

"Hold up, Nasty, I wanted to kick it with you. It's been a minute since I've seen you," Marla said in a desperate attempt to calm things down.

"And it'll be a minute before y'all see me again." He got up to leave. Von had tears in her eyes. They never argued before. She didn't mean to call him soft, but she was used to him ready to bust his guns for her, and she felt like the world had abandoned her. She felt she'd become a burden. This disease was getting to her. And she thought about walking out of the prison and walking right into fast-moving traffic. Nobody knew what she was going through inside. Not even her brother.

CHAPTER 8

"Tony, what are you doing here?" his cousin asked him.

"I just need a little something to get me started."

"Tone, man, you're speaking out of pure heartache. Drugs have never been part of your résumé, dawg. You don't even know how to cut dope, so I know good and well you don't know shit about running no block and selling it." Tony went to his cousin Biggie trying to get him to sell him some work so he could step his game up. Paige looked so happy sitting in the company of a man who could take care of her better than he could. And when Marla called him broke, that was just too much for him. She not only embarrassed him, but she was sitting up under a cat getting major money. Mad-Dog was known all over Baltimore and beyond.

Mad-Dog had a gang of loyal dudes on his team from McCabe and East Baltimore. And Tony knew that the name Mad-Dog was a title that spoke for itself. At all costs, Tony wanted to avoid a war with Mad-Dog, at least until his pockets were thick enough to wage war on his own.

Tony loved Paige and their daughter Tonaya with all his heart. She was damn near named after him. He knew he fucked up, but Paige never gave him a chance to explain himself. If it took the glamorous life to pull her back in, then so be it. He didn't care what he had to do. The only issue he had right now was convincing his cousin Biggie to put him on and finding a few loyal thugs to rock with him.

"Listen, if I'ma spend my last, I'd rather spend it with you, fam. But if you don't wanna help a brother out, I'll go elsewhere."

"So you really serious about this, huh?"

"As a stroke!"

"I don't feel right putting you on. You've managed to stay out of the streets, and now you wanna get involved because of your pride? I think you need to think about it."

"No disrespect, cuzzo, but I'm a grown-ass man. Paige on some bullshit. She moved out of the house and not fuckin' with me at all. I haven't seen Tonaya. I quit my job. I got a lot of shit going on, and I need to make this happen. So either you're with me or against me."

"Well, I'm definitely not against you. Let me tell you something. I got in the game the same exact way. My baby mama started fucking with Mike Regents from the Ravens. I was like, oh, hell, no. This nigga not about to be buying my daughter better gifts than me. That was 10 years ago. So I can relate. It's a pride thing. But I've missed not one, but two federal indictments by the skin of my ass. So just know what you're getting yourself into."

"I'm not gonna stay in long. I'ma just get in, make some paper, and get out."

"Sounds good, Tony. But the game is a drug itself. You think the fiends are the only ones that get addicted? Nah, *we're* the real addicts."

"I managed to stay out of the game all this time. Six months max."

"Okay. Whatever you say, cuz. But if you're gonna do this, be smart. Get a young worker and let his name claim the fame. You keep your name on the low." Tony was listening, but not really. The whole point of this was to make money and show that he could compete with Mad-Dog. His cousin didn't grab his attention until he started explaining the game to him.

"When can I get that work?"

"Slow down, Pablo. For the next 2 weeks, it's me and you. I'ma school you. You'll get Hustle Game 101. I'ma show you how to run your own block," Biggie said.

"A'ight, bet."

For the next 2 weeks Biggie did just that. He explained to his cousin everything he needed to know about the dope crowd, how to cut it up, give out testers before opening up shop, and how to protect his territory. Those 2 weeks were the most intense 2 weeks of Tony's life. It revealed to him how fast the paper could come rolling in. Money wasn't the only thing that was fast . . . so was Tony's ability to pick up the game. He was very intelligent, so he was able to figure a few things out on his own. Biggie was impressed.

Tony went out and got six young cats to work the block for him. He got an apartment to trap out of a week later. Biggie couldn't believe it. Tony was moving 200 grams a day after cutting it. His listened to Biggie and let his name stay on the low for the time being. But it wasn't for the reasons Biggie gave him; it was because he didn't want to be known as a small-timer once his name got out there. Once he got his shit right, muh'fuckas was gon' know 'bout Tony!

Tony did not intend to mess around with Sharise. He went out and shopped for Paige and Tonaya for Christmas, and he was upset that he couldn't buy them the kind of things he felt they deserved. So his homeboy introduced him to Sharise and said she was the connect on everything. Sharise was a street chick. She boosted clothes and sold a little weed and crack every now and then. She was kind of cute, and he flirted with her with intentions on getting a discount on a couple of things, but it went too far. He didn't mean for it to destroy his relationship with Paige, not at all.

He was putting some time in with Sharise, and on a drunk night, ended up sleeping with her. But his feelings weren't in it. Sharise liked Tony a lot more than he liked her. But because of Paige kicking it with Mad-Dog and her shutting him out, he found himself in Sharise's company much more than he should have been. He was hurt, and he blamed all of his troubles on the lack of money.

As the weeks rolled on by, Tony was coming up. He had his block on smash and even had to get four more young dudes to work for him. He was making a few dollars. But nothing stayed secret in the hood. One day, he was coming off his block, and Rodney waved him down. He pulled over.

"Tony, whattup, baby? I see you over here rolling now."

"Nah, don't let nobody fool you. I'm not making any noise."

"That's good. Keep it like that. Rats is running wild in the city, telling everything they heard and some mo' shit these days."

"Most definitely. But you know, I stay to myself and fucks with myself, so any problems I got, it's with myself, ya hear?"

"I like that philosophy," Rodney stated. Rod could tell Tony was getting his hands dirty now. He looked like new money and even bought a new vocabulary. Usually Tony talked a li'l more proper, but he was dropping street

Ebonics. Yeah, he was into something new. Suddenly, Star sat up. She had been in Rodney's lap the whole time. This nicca was crazy, Tony thought. She got out of the car and ran into the corner store.

"Gottdamn, my nicca, Shorty still illegal, ain't she?" Tony asked.

"Illegal to buy liquor, but not illegal to take dick. Baby girl bleeding and coming like a grown woman," Rodney said proudly.

"You wildin', Rod. You better leave them young chicks alone. Your ass gon' have bad luck."

"I got too much money to have bad luck. I can buy good fortune, baby."

Tony just shook his head. "So what's up with Von? How she doing?"

"You tell me. I haven't seen her ass. She call herself being mad at me. She packed herself and moved out. I figure she probably staying with you and Paige."

"Nah, Paige ain't fucking with me right now. I got caught up with Sharise on some bullshit, and Paige found out. She bounced on me. So I haven't seen her or my daughter. I thought maybe she was staying with y'all."

"Damn, we all fucked up, huh? But they'll be back."

"I don't know. Maybe Von, but Paige is taking it a little bit too far. She been kicking it wit' ol' boy Mad-Dog."

"Say, word? Damn, Tone. That's foul. I better not find

out Von on no bullshit."

"Well, they been all hanging out on Friday's at Hammers. You might find her there."

"For her sake, I hope I don't."

"Since I got you right here, let me ask you a question, Rod. You already got a banging spot up top, so whattup with letting me open up on the block with this dope I got? You know, the more fiends, the more money. We can work something out."

Rod tilted his head from side to side contemplating. "You know what, Tone, that's not a bad idea. We'll talk about that later. My peoples is coming, so I'll holla at you." Just then the young girl came out of the store and got back in the car with Rod. He drove off after dapping with Tony. When Rodney drove off, he couldn't help himself. His mind was focused on Von. All he could think about was her fucking with one of Mad-Dog's boys following behind Paige. Hell, no. That was *not* an option. He wasn't going out like that. There was no way that shit was going down.

Tony was making moves. He learned quickly that a closed mouth doesn't get fed. He was talking to cats and asking discreet questions about what spots were available. He located three vacant streets in East Baltimore that nobody was claiming, and he proceeded to set up shop. It seemed like Tony's business was growing by the minute. He was happy that things were moving along. Soon, Paige wouldn't be able to deny his status.

He went to the mall and picked up a few things for Tonaya. He missed his baby girl, and by hook or crook, he was gonna see his daughter and spend time with her.

Sharise thought Tony was just something fun to do. She didn't expect this new Tony. She saw his drive and how he was starting to come up in the game. She was going to back away from Tony at first, but after seeing how he was moving some numbers, she decided to stick around. She felt like she could be the brains behind Tony's operation. Sharise wanted to get on herself, but nobody would put her on because she had too many snake qualities. Everybody liked buying shit from a thief, but nobody wanted to do business with one. So she saw Tony as an opportunity to come up, and she didn't plan on going anywhere!

CHAPTER 9

"Dr. Maru, are you sure?" Von asked as she sat back on the examination table.

"Yes."

"I just can't believe this. Does this happen to people with this disease?"

"The normal ones, but this is indeed rare," the doctor said. "You can get dressed now." The doctor's latex gloves went into the trash, and she marked a few things on Von's chart. Then she turned around and smiled at her, but Von didn't see anything that was worth smiling about. Not in her predicament.

"Here is a new prescription fill." The doctor scribbled her name and ripped a prescription order off of a pad.

"Do I have to take it every day? Will it make me sick?" Von asked.

"You might feel a little queasy, but anything more than that, let me know right away, okay? And I need you to come back next week so we can make the best decision on what we're going to do. This is so rare, but I'll sit with my team and try to figure out the best option for you."

Von began to cry. This couldn't be happening. This disease wasn't just bad, it was the devil himself manifesting as a horrible sickness in her very own body.

"I just feel so dirty. So nasty inside. I don't understand how this could happen. Just when I thought it couldn't get worse."

"Your medicine seems to be working, Von. I'm here for you. You call my office anytime. And you also have my cell phone. Use it for any emergency, okay? We're going to take care of you. We'll do all we can. Preservation of life is our main objective."

Von nodded and wiped the tears that fell from her eyes.

"I want you to call Dr. Harmond. He's a psychologist over at Howard. He can help you get through this. You call him anytime and tell him I referred you, okay?" Dr. Maru felt bad for Von. The last few years she'd witnessed an epidemic. AIDS was claiming so many young lives. Most of the cases were young African Americans. It was a sad thing to see. But she dedicated her life to helping.

Von walked into the house crying after going to the doctor. Her face was swollen and tearstained. She wouldn't allow Marla or Paige to go with her whenever she went to the doctor. Paige put little Tonaya down onto the carpet and ran to her friend. The tears rolling down Von's face scared both Marla and Paige.

"What's wrong?" Paige asked. Marla got her some tissue. Von let out a vicious cry that felt like a sharp pain to both her girls.

"Things just get worse and worse by the fucking minute." Neither one of her friends could figure out what was wrong. She already started her medicine, and the bad news had already been as bad as it could get, right? So what could it be now? They were already dealing with Von being HIV-positive. They were already dealing with cloudy days no matter how bright the sun shined. So whatever this was, it had to be bad.

They waited for Von to calm down. "What happened? Tell us," Marla asked softly.

"My doctor's appointment. It wasn't good."

"Well, what happened? What do you mean it wasn't good?" They were hoping that her doctor hadn't given her a time line left to live or no crazy shit like that. Von caught the disease early, and her prognosis was that she might be able to live a normal life for a long time. They didn't understand what caused so much despair at this moment. But then again, neither of them were dealing with such a devastating illness; they were both on the outside looking in. Having HIV wasn't just about the sickness itself. It was the stigma that came with it that was even worse than the disease. People were uneducated about it, and that caused them to say the wildest things. They did their best to protect Von from that, and it helped that nobody knew besides them.

Von dropped to the floor, and her girls sat beside her.

"Tell us, boo. You know we are here for you, no matter what."

"I know. But this, this was just so unexpected. I found out today that I'm pregnant. Almost 3 months."

"Oh my God. Von!" Paige said.

"I had no idea. I thought my body changing was because of the medicine or my illness. I had no idea I was pregnant."

"That's great. We get to spoil another baby!" Marla said, hugging her. She was all smiles . . . until she saw the look on Paige's face. Then she backed up. "Wait a minute, can it pass to the baby?" Paige gave her another look. Sometimes Marla spoke without thinking. Paige's expression clearly was saying for Marla to use her damn brain about now.

"That's what I am scared of. The medicine is doing its job. My blood work came back showing that the virus was undetected."

"That's great! Oh my God! It's a miracle!" Marla said. Paige just shook her head.

"That doesn't mean I'm cured. It's just the medicine doing its job. There is a 50–50 chance that the baby could get it. All I can do is pray."

"Well, we'll be praying right with you," Paige added.

"I wish I never met Rod. I hate him. He's not only condemned me, but his children too. Why did I have to be with a no-good man like him? I should have listened to Nasty and stayed away from him back then."

"Girl, his ass manipulated you. You weren't out looking for him or trying to be grown like I was," Marla said. She made Von smile. "You were all into school, and he kept coming onto you. Buying you shit, calling you, treating you like his girl before you were. Who wouldn't have fallen for that?"

"You got a point, I guess, but I still should have listened to Nasty. I hate fighting with him. He hasn't called me or nothing."

"You know he's stubborn."

"So how soon before you find out the sex of the baby?"

"I'm not even thinking about that right now. I just want the best for my baby. I want him or her to be healthy, you know?"

"It will all work out. Don't worry about it."

Just then, the baby started crying. "Sounds like somebody is hungry," Paige said, picking up her two-year-old. Little Tonaya was adorable.

"I want Daddy," she said, clear as day. Silence filled the room. "Where Daddy?" she asked in her innocent voice.

"Daddy is working." Paige put Tonaya down, and her little feet took off running. Then she came back carrying her mother's cell phone. She put in her lap and waited. Then she looked up at her mother as if to say, *What the hell is taking you so long? Call him!*

"You better call Tony," Von said.

"No!"

"You ain't right. You can't keep that man's daughter from him," Marla added.

"I'm not trying to, but I don't want my daughter around that ho, Sharise. And I know he is still messing with her because I did a drive-by 2 days ago, and he was at her house."

"You know where she lives?"

"Yes, I did a reverse search from the phone number. His car was in her driveway."

"Dirty!"

"Dirty isn't the word. But . . . You're right. He is her father. I have to figure out something."

"I hate to think that this will be my life," Von said. "No offense to you, Paige, but just to know that I may have to deal with Rodney for the rest of my life makes me sick. I don't wanna have to see his face. And this baby is going to change that. I won't have a choice. I won't keep him from his baby, but, damn! It will be like the nightmare that never ends."

"Yes, and your baby father is the real Freddie Krueger." They all started laughing.

Von had a lot to think about. And seeing the pleading look on Tonaya's face and how she craved her father let her know that keeping Rod out of her baby's life was unthinkable. She grew up without parents, and she wanted her baby to have a better life than she did. It wasn't going to be easy, but she would find a way to make everything gel together as best she could.

"When are you going to tell Rodney?" Paige asked.

"I don't know. But I have to tell him. I'll tell him soon."

"About everything, right? You can't keep it from him, Von."

"I know. I won't. I'll tell that bastard. And maybe he'll drop dead on the spot and save me a lot of time and energy."

CHAPTER 10

Word got to Rodney that Moon was looking for him. Moon left a number where he could be reached at any time. Rodney just got finished breaking down 10 kilos into smaller quantities of weight and cooking up two for his men. He was busy and couldn't figure out why Moon wanted him. He thought that maybe Moon changed his mind on being his shooter. But even if he did, after the way he spoke to Rod, the offer was off the table. The only thing they had in common was that he was Nasty's man, and he was in a relationship with Nasty's little sister.

The story on the streets was that Nasty and Soulja had put in some work in Brazil to avenge Nasty's parents' death. And once they got there, the girl that set up the trip had set them up. Some Brazilian gangbangers held court with fully automatic weapons, but Soulja and Nasty were not easy targets. Not only did they escape, but they made off with some fresh Brazilian cocaine. But somebody set them up. Turns out, it was Soulja's girl. That's what the streets say. And when they got back, they both were arrested.

Rod took a break and went into a back room and dialed Moon. He answered on the forth ring. "Moon, whattup? This Rod."

"I was expecting your call. Nasty asked me to get in touch with you. He said you need to come and see him on Saturday, by yourself."

"Something up?" Rod asked curiously.

"I don't know the details. I'm just passing a message."

"A'ight, cool. Tell him I'll be there bright and early."

"Make sure it's after eleven after he make his rounds."

"So I'm on Nasty's time now, huh? 'Cause, really, I—"

Moon cut him off. "I'm in the middle of something!" Moon hung up without warning. He wasn't about to get into a tongue struggle with Rod, and he hung up before Rod said something that warranted a hit. Moon knew that Rod must have already crossed some type of line if Nasty was requesting to see him. It was most likely about Von. And everybody knew that Nasty didn't play when it came to his sister. Whatever it was Rod had done couldn't have been that bad because Nasty had ordered a meeting rather than a hit.

He went back to cleaning and oiling his arsenal and waited for a call from Nasty in case anything went wrong, even though the odds of that were slim because everybody acted like Nasty and Soulja were ghosts. And they still feared the ghosts years later as though they never left.

Rodney went to the crib. The house looked the same, except he didn't smell Von's perfume. Her clothes were not in the closet. The bed was not made. He had hoped that she would have come home, even just to talk, but she didn't. She was not answering her phone. She was not calling him back. Nothing. And he could not find her. He picked up the phone and dialed the young girl he caught walking home the other day. He invited her over. Excited, the young girl walked over to the place that Rod and Von had once called home. When the girl rang the bell, Rod sniffed a few lines, and then ran to open the door.

The girl walked in. She couldn't have been older than 14. Rod pulled her close to him.

"How did you get so beautiful?"

She giggled. "You got a nice house."

"I'm glad you like it. I got you something."

"Me?"

"Yeah, I just wanna make sure I got the right size. Let me guess, you wear a seven shoe."

"Seven and a half," she said. "But I can fit a seven, depending on what it is." Rod opened the closet behind him and took out a brand-new pair of Jordans. They were Von's, but she'd never worn them. They were brand new. He passed them to the young girl.

"Here," he said.

"Oh my God. These are the vintage ones. I love these. Thank you." He snatched them back. She frowned. "I can't have them?" she asked, disappointed.

"Of course, you can. But when you got a grown-ass man like me ready to take care of you, you gotta be a grown-ass woman."

"I can be a grown-ass woman. Everybody says I don't look my age anyway," she said.

"You got hair on that pussy?" he asked.

"Yeah, a little bit."

"Let me see it."

"Umm . . ." the girl said hesitating.

"See what I'm saying? You're not read to be a grown woman yet. You're playing games."

"No, I am ready." She unbuttoned her pants and dropped them to the floor. She stood there in her panties.

"Take those off too," Rod said. She did as she was told. Her young body did something to Rod. His dick immediately got hard. "Come here," he said to her. She walked over to him covering herself. Rod moved her hands and began playing with her clit. The young girl felt things she'd never felt before. But Rod noticed she was extra timid, and he didn't have time for this shit.

"Can I go now?" she asked.

"Why you acting so shy?"

"I'm a virgin." Rod's eyes grew so large they almost

popped out of his head. The thought of young tightness aroused him greatly.

"Lie down," he said.

"But I don't want to!"

Rod was tired of playing with her. He forced her on the bed, and out of fear, she opened her legs to him. He didn't take his time or try to be gentle with the young girl; instead, he entered her as though the girl had been with him many times before. She bled as he pushed his way inside. And he began thrusting and pumping. The disease leaked from him into the innocent. When he was done with her, he kissed her. She left his house with a brand-new pair of Jordans . . . and a brand-new illness.

Saturday at noon, Nasty was called to the visiting room. Moon had informed him a couple of days earlier that Rod would be coming to visit.

Rod walked into the prison, but he got a surprise. Marla. Marla happened to show up by sheer coincidence, and she refused to leave. So the two of them signed in at the same time to see Nasty. When Nasty walked out, he was thrown off by seeing Marla.

"What are you doing here, Marla? You know I don't play that coming to see me without telling me first."

"Nicca, you better kiss me right now!" she said. She

gave him a look, and he knew she was holding something. He wasn't expecting this, and the guard on duty was not someone on his payroll. So when she passed Nasty the package, he swallowed it. He'd throw it up later.

"You need to leave, Marla," Nasty said.

"I came up here to handle business for you, and you're dismissing me?" she said with an attitude.

"I need to talk to this man in private." Nasty saw how disappointed Marla looked so he softened up a li'l bit. "Okay, look, go in the kids' room over there and watch *Sesame Street* or some shit for a half hour. I need to talk to this man."

Marla did as Nasty said.

"You look good, Nasty. How you holding up?" Rod asked. He peeped how Nasty was looking. He was in the best shape of his life.

"How are you and your men doing?" Nasty asked Rod, ignoring his compliment. It was his turn to play the last Don, and Rod peeped it.

"We're doing better than most. I can't complain," Rod said.

"That's good."

"So what is this urgent request all about? Moon made it sound like there was an issue or something. You need me to handle something for you?"

"There is one thing that will make me turn my city red,

and that's my sister. I know money make a man forget what's important to him or what should be important to him. Von came to see me not too long ago, and she spoke very negatively about you. I could see the hurt in her face, and I need to know why Von's heart is so broken."

"Yo, Nasty, real talk, I haven't seen Von in over a month. She's been ducking me, and it's driving me crazy. She moved out in the middle of the night or some shit. And I haven't seen her at all."

"Don't play dumb, my nigga. She's been ducking you for a reason. She's tired of going through it with you, so she's done with you. So let me be clear. I'm through with you for her. My sister ain't nobody's dog. I respected you for picking up my weight after I fell and making sure Von was good. For that alone, I come to you in peace," Nasty said.

"I love Von. You know I do. I can make it up to her. Every man makes mistakes. She probably found out I was messing around a little bit. But I was just having a little bit of fun. I'm not trying to ruin what I have with Von. I bought her a ring not too long ago."

"Well, you fucked up, and she's done."

"Listen, I can make it up to her. 'Cause let me honest. I will kill before I see her with someone else," Rod admitted.

"I'm being kind. But you will do as I say, yo. It's a wrap for you and my sister. It's over. She's done, and so am I. When you see Von, you speak and keep it moving. People call me and Von twins because we share the same soul. That's my baby girl. And she hurt—so I'm hurt. You might kill for her, but I will wage a war in her honor. I'll take out mothers, grandmothers, sisters, nephews, and whoever else need to go to right the wrongs done to her. That's a great price to pay for love when you can find it somewhere else. Like I said, my respect remains intact. Let's keep it that way, soldier."

Rodney was steaming on the inside. Who the fuck did Nasty think he was? "Listen—" Rodney said.

"Listen nothing."

"A'ight. I guess that's law, then," Rod said. Most OG meetings like this were called to keep peace in the streets. Rod wanted to tell Nasty go fuck himself, but he knew that Nasty had too much respect in the streets still, and all he had to do was make a phone call and a war would be started with Rod and his crew. He wasn't trying to go there, at least not yet.

"You be safe out there, Rod. And here is some advice . . . You made a name for yourself, and that's not good," Nasty said before standing up. "You need to bring it down a few notches."

"I hear you, Nasty. I'll do that." Rod extended his hand to dap with Nasty, but instead of extending his hand back, Nasty pat him on the shoulder and sent him off. Rod's mouth twisted in a knot. He felt as though Nasty insulted him.

As Rodney left the prison, wild thoughts ran through his head. Who the hell was Nasty to tell him who he could be with? Von was grown, and so was he. He could make his own decisions. And why the fuck was Von coming up to the prison and telling Nasty their business in the first place? There had been several occasions that he wanted to slap the hell out of Von, but he didn't because he knew she might tell her brother. But at this point, it didn't even matter. If he heard even the slightest word that Von was fucking with somebody else, he would put all his worries about war to the side and let bullets fly where they may. When it came to what was his, he had no limits. If it came down to it, he'd fight for what he felt belonged to him.

Rodney drove out of the prison parking lot vexed. He called his man Black and told him to send a message to Shorty 55. Shorty 55 had been locked up for 20 damn years, at this very same prison. He used to get his work from Rod, but he slowed up. Rod told his man Black to let Shorty 55 know that it was time he stepped his game up in the prison. Rod wanted to let Nasty know that he didn't run everything. He had power too.

CHAPTER 11

"So you're pursuing your singing, huh, Keva?" Soulja said to his girl over the phone. Keva was taking care of I'sa, Soulja's daughter, after her mother got killed. She stepped up. And even though Keva was just somebody who Soulja was dealing with because she came with certain benefits, she took on a major role in his life. Taking care of his daughter was more than he could have ever asked for. And with him serving a life sentence, there was no better way to show loyalty to him. So he married her while he was in prison and took care of her as if she was the love of his life.

"Yeah, I booked a gig at Club Milan. I'm singing there tomorrow night."

"Just be safe out there."

"I will. I heard from Nasty earlier. He called to talk to I'sa. He's such a good uncle to her."

"Yeah, he is. And he'll be checking on y'all all the time. He got a crack law reduction that had been due to him a long time ago, and he just got the two-point reduction. So he'll be home soon. And he's gonna be in her life. I've been putting together the plan for him to come home and stay legit. I'm happy about that. I can live through him."

Keva didn't want to talk about Soulja not coming home. She didn't think it was fair that Nasty was coming home and Soulja wasn't. But Soulja took the charge for the bodies, and Nasty went down for the drugs. Soulja felt it didn't make sense for them both to do life. Keva respected it and hated it at the same time.

He could hear his daughter in the background.

"Mommy is that Daddy?" she asked. Keva was the only mother she knew.

"Yes, come talk to him, baby." He could hear her little footsteps running to the phone.

"Daddy!" she said. The sound of her voice warmed his heart.

"What's up, baby?"

"Daddy, I had a dream you came home! You was here to take me to kindergarten on my first day."

Soulja closed his eyes and fought back the tears. "I am gonna be there. I'm gonna be invisible, though. I'll be watching you to make sure nobody bothers you."

"Nobody is gonna bother me, Daddy. I know how to fight. Remember on the visit you showed me how to punch. I punched this boy in my pre-k class just like that."

"You did? Did he cry?"

"Yuup, just like a li'l girl."

Soulja busted out laughing. His li'l princess was the most precious thing in the world to him. He tried everything in his power to instill things in her from a distance. She was all the good in him. *BEEP BEEP*. The 1-minute warning made itself known.

"Okay, put your mom back on the phone. I'll call you tomorrow, baby."

"But we didn't even talk for 5 minutes."

"I know, but we will tomorrow. I need to talk to your mother. I love you. Keva, you there?"

"Yeah, I'm here."

"Okay, bring her up here next weekend. I need to see my baby."

"Just her?" Keva said.

"Come on now. You know I need to see you too. My *wife*."

"I love you."

"I love you too, baby," he said. He loved her because of the way she stepped up and stayed loyal. He couldn't ask for more. The phone disconnected, and Soulja met up with Nasty. They had some business to tend to. Soulja walked over to Nasty's room to kick it with him.

"Whattup, Soulja?" Nasty said. His eyes were glazed.

"What's wrong with you, fam?"

"I just finished throwing up. I had to get that shit up out of me. Marla slid me something on the visit and I had to swallow that shit quick. I wasn't expecting her to show up."

"I thought you was kicking it with Rod," Soulja asked.

"I was, but she showed up by coincidence. Damn, I felt like I was gagging forever."

Soulja laughed at his man and left to get him a glass of water. Clean water, boiled in the kitchen. He said he'd be back in about 10 minutes. Right after he left, Rocky, one of their trusted workers, walked into the cell.

"Yo, Shorty 55 is outside your cell. He wants to come in and talk to you."

"Shorty 55? Fuck he want?" Nasty asked.

Rocky shrugged his shoulders. "I don't know. But he's not alone."

"Pat him down and send him in," Nasty instructed.

Shorty 55 walked in. Nasty stood up. "Whattup?" Nasty said.

"Yo, I'm hip to you and your li'l men hitting the visiting room real nice. Not once have any of you sent me a bag of work—dust, nothing. That's unheard of in this prison. Everybody hits Shorty 55 when that thing land." He heard about them getting work in because Shorty 55 was one of Rodney's homeboys.

"Look 55, I been in this jail for 5 years. And not once has a nigga ever tried to press me no kind of way. I don't owe nobody shit. And I'm the one hitting yo. My li'l men ain't got shit to do with this," Nasty said.

"I don't care how long you've been here. I'm sick of hearing about y'all, and I can't get my nose dirty. You gotta respect dudes like me, Nasty. I been running this spot forever."

Nasty laughed. This infuriated Shorty 55.

"I heard about you, but apparently you haven't heard about *me*," Nasty said.

"It don't work like that behind these walls, dawg. This is *my* world, and what *I* say goes . . . or the individual goes."

Nasty was vexed. Suddenly, two big burly-ass dudes appeared in front of the doorway. Shorty 55 was coming at him like he was a sucker.

"You must not know who the fuck you talking to, dawg." Nasty said.

"This *my* world, youngin'. And you gotta respect dudes like me. That's just the way it is. I made it possible for cats like you to even get money up in here."

Nasty was pissed. He couldn't believe Shorty 55 was coming at him like he was a sucker. He was far from press material. He wanted to bust off on 55 right there, but yo had two, jive, big-ass muh'fuckas with him, and Nasty was by himself since Soulja had stepped away. Knowing Soulja, he stopped and was kicking it with Mo Garrett on his way back. Nasty was a beast when it came to brawling. But it would be stupid to kick shit off, one to three. He wasn't stupid. So he played Shorty 55's game.

"Look, OG, I respect where you're coming from. But if you want my product, make sure your money is straight," Nasty said.

"So, you gon' force my hand, huh, Nasty?"

"Slim, I told you what it was. I'll bless you with some work. I'll even give you a discount. But you gotta pay like everybody else."

"I'm jive fucked up you disregarding who I am, but sometimes you gotta hand a nigga his shit in blood so he know his spills just like the next man. I hope you'll sleep on my humble approach."

"And I hope you'll do the same with my offer," Nasty said.

Just then Soulja walked in.

"Just hold some of that blow for me. It won't take me long to get my money right." 55 and his men walked off.

"Yo, what the fuck is up with that clown?" Soulja asked.

"He must be smoking if he thought he could press me about some dope," Nasty said.

"Oh yeah, that's what Slim wanted?" Soulja said curiously, setting the water down on the table.

"Wanting and getting is two different things," Nasty added.

"Yo, we gotta watch that nigga," Rocky said now walking into the room joining them. Nasty and Soulja knew many dudes would come to the window and call out to 55 from the street, but they were a bunch of low-level-nothing cats. He never thought that he would approach him like this. Not if he valued his life.

"Go get Mo Garrett for me," Nasty ordered. Rocky left and was back with Mo Garrett in a jiff.

"What's going on in here?" Mo said. He had on gloves and boots with shorts on. Soulja started laughing.

"Where you was going, Mo?" Nasty asked.

"I came ready to stomp some ass. Rocky came in my room like there was a problem. I'm always ready," he said as he made a karate stance. Even Nasty had to laugh because Mo was dead-ass serious. He loved them and would die for them in heartbeat if it came down to it. "What's going on up in here?" he asked with a serious look on his face.

"That cat 55 stepped to me today trying to put his soft press game down," Nasty said.

"Here we go! I expected this years ago, but it never came. That cat is a sucker," Mo Garrett said. "And I know you told him he need to come correct."

"You know I did. I ain't never had to worry about being pressed."

"And you shouldn't have to. I'ma have a word with him. But I know this dude well. If he thinks he can run through you, he'll come at you and your crew strong. And you don't need that, son. You're about to get out of here if your two-points come through. We need you out there. We got bigger plans than some jailhouse beef over some dope."

"I understand that, but if he comes at me, I'ma hit back with something way more powerful."

"Let me handle it, son," Mo said.

"Yeah, let Mo handle it his way first," Soulja added.

Nasty spun around and looked at Soulja like he had two heads. Usually Soulja was the one ready to snap a nigga's head in two. Nasty was taken aback by Soulja's calmness. But Soulja wanted their business priorities to stay most important. This clown 55 wasn't worth their time.

Mo put his hand on Soulja's shoulder. "Yes, I'll do it *my* way first. And then if he still wants a problem, I'll put my stomping boots back on. And I don't trust his ass. He might drop a dime to the police, so let me hold the work just in case there's a raid."

"I know, Mo, good idea. You are always thinking ahead, and that's why I got a ton of respect for you. I know we have plans, and hopefully, we won't have to go there, but on everything I love, if he come at my brother foul again, and he wants to wage war . . . I'll remind him why they call me Soulja in the first place."

CHAPTER 12

Von sat in church with her mind made up that she was ready for change. She didn't know what else to do. She was over the whole idea that she couldn't do anything and had to just hope for the best. She figured that God had to have a say.

"Is there anyone in here that don't know God and wants to accept the Lord into their life?"

Von didn't know where else to turn. She'd always heard that the church was the only way to get your life right. To get your blessings. So she wanted to do just that. And just maybe her baby would be born healthy. Von raised her hand.

"Come on up here, young lady. God loves you and knows your troubles. What's your name?" the preacher asked.

"Shavon Jones ."

"God bless you, Shavon. And I ask the Lord to come into your life. Renew your spirit so that you can be blessed. Do you accept the Lord as your Savior?"

"I do," Von said, not really sure if this was the right thing to do. But she felt out of options. Von repeated every word the preacher said, blindly. But still, she was leaning on a man for guidance rather than leaning on herself and her own intellect. But desperate people do desperate things.

"Amen," the preacher said. He walked Von down the three steps descending from the altar, and she made her way back to her seat. But when she looked up, she got the shock of her life. Rodney was sitting in her same pew smiling at her.

"Baby, can we talk?"

"No, Rod. We can talk after the service."

He waited. He normally wouldn't, but he was so happy to see Von, he'd wait a lifetime. When the service was over, they walked outside together. In front of the church was a brand-new X6 that Rod bought for her. There was a white bow on top. He dangled the keys in front of her face.

"Von, I bought you a new car. You deserve it, baby." He didn't understand why she was at church in the first place. It gave him the creeps.

"I don't want your car, Rodney. I'm waiting on Marla to pick me up."

"Hold up a minute, baby. You just disappear on me, then jump headfirst into church. What's going on, baby?"

"My life needs a change. A *major* change. And you helped me see just how valuable my life is. I gave you my heart, my virginity, my loyalty—my everything. You were my everything, Rod. You were my god at one time, so I needed to come to church and find a God who is worthy of the title. Because you are not."

"I had to damn near threaten somebody to find out where you were."

"Well, I'm kind of glad you are here because there is something I need to tell you."

Rodney noticed how soft spoken she was. How her face had taken on an angelic glow. He almost felt bad for doing her so wrong.

"What is it?" he asked taking a step closer to her. "I love you, Von. We can get through whatever."

"I'm pregnant, Rod." His jaw dropped. He couldn't believe what she just told him. Pregnant! He smiled. Not so much because he was about to become a father, but because he suddenly felt back in charge of things. Even if she didn't want anything to do with him, he was always going to be part of her life as her baby father. He would get back close to her by being an excellent pops and being there for her like never before.

"Word, Von? So I'm about to be a father? Baby, that's beautiful. The best part is that *you* are the mother. I swear to you, Von, I'm gonna do right by you. I'ma take care of y'all," he said excitedly.

She smiled at him and tilted her head to the side. "You better hope this baby doesn't come out HIV-positive."

Rodney stepped back. "What? Why the fuck you would you say something like that? How in the hell could something like that happen?"

"How you think, Rodney? *You* passed that shit to me! I'm 18 years old and got bigger problems than I can handle. Your money, your cars, your words, none of that can save me—or your baby, Rod. And it's all because of your carelessness and disrespect. I guess this is *your* Karma."

Rodney's world was shaken. Von had delivered a Mike Tyson blow to his dome. "Please tell me you're joking, Von. Please!"

"Do I look like I'm joking? How many young girls' lives have you ruined out there? How many?" A tear fell from her eye. "You need to let all them females you were cheating on me with know that they need to get checked. If you don't, *I* will. You destroyed so many lives. So many."

"Somebody had to give me the shit, Von. Goddamn, you act like *I* created the disease or something. Fuck!" he said rubbing his head from back to front. Then he put both of his hands on top of his head and let his hands rest there. "This can't be. This can't."

"That's how I felt. Now I got it, and your baby might have it too."

He blew out a breath of air. "What the fuck I'm 'posed to do now, Von? Does your brother know about this shit?" he asked.

"No! Hell, no! Nasty can never know. He has too many

problems as it is." Just then, Marla and Paige pulled up. She got in the car.

"Fuck I'm supposed to do now?" he said, grabbing Von's arm before she got in the car.

"Talk to God!" she said before climbing in and driving off with her girls.

"What the hell did his ass want, Von?"

"A miracle. I told him he was gave me HIV."

"Oh shit. You told him?"

"I had to. And you should have seen him. He looked like a hopeless child."

"He lucky it wasn't me telling him because I'd report his ass to the board of health," Paige said.

"Hell, yeah," Marla added.

"I'm not worried about that. I'm more concerned with my baby. But if I find out he's not telling the girls he had sex with, I *will* report him. He is handing out death sentences, you might as well say."

"You ain't never lied, girl, and God forbid if Nasty or Soulja finds out. His ass won't last to even die from the disease."

"Y'all keep talking about dying, but the medicine today is amazing."

"Sometimes it works; sometimes it doesn't. That's not the point. I've seen lots of people die from it. I always thought it was just dope fiends and prostitutes or gay men that got it.

But I was so wrong. I was a virgin when I got with Rod, stayed with only one man, and look what happened."

That silenced Paige and Marla. They'd both been with men unprotected, and they realized how serious Von's point was. Von spoke again. She was learning to accept the disease more and more each day. Sadness or denial wouldn't cure her.

"My brother will never know about this. He couldn't handle it. And I want him to be happy with Marla. I want you guys to work out. I can't have my issues blocking your happiness," Von said. Paige and Marla were moved by Von's selflessness.

"You don't have to worry about us saying anything to Nasty. Lips are sealed!"

Marla and Paige both knew that if they said anything to Nasty and leaked that kind of information, they would be cut off for life. And neither one of them could live with that.

"Our friendships are based on trust. It stands on y'all word."

"You don't even have to go that far and say that, Von. You already know that your secret is safe here. We love you to death, and if you don't want it mentioned to Nasty, it surely won't come from us."

CHAPTER 13

Mo Garrett sat in his sell counting the $10 bags of raw that he just got from Nasty and Soulja. They both went on a visit. He made sure the workers were on top of things for his sons in their absence. One of Soulja's regulars came in and bought a $20 bag of blow. Mo put the money to the side to give to Nasty later.

Mo Garrett was well respected. He had the prison on lock with both poker games and the gambling scene. He had at least 300 cartons of cigarettes in five different cells. The correction pigs wouldn't fuck with his business because he kept everybody happy. He schooled both Soulja and Nasty on how to get money behind the wall. Everybody loved Mo Garrett. There was nobody on his side of the prison that couldn't get fair action on a couple of grams of dope or whatever he had on credit. He had established a lot of respect and love because he wasn't a petty dude, and he let men eat who had no other means to survive.

Mo closed the door to his cell and dumped the 50 bags of blow on his bed. As usual, Rocky stood watch. But suddenly, Mo Garrett heard shuffling outside his cell. He called out to Rocky but didn't get a response. He pulled a sheet over the dope and slipped his feet into his ass-stomping boots. As soon as Mo Garrett opened his door to step out of his cell, he was bum-rushed by a bunch of dudes wearing bandannas around their faces. They all had knives and shanks that looked like they were used for carving up cattle—or niggers, for that matter. In walked Shorty 55 and stood in front of his men.

"Where the dope at, Mo? Don't play Superman or your ass might end up in a wheelchair just like him," Shorty 55 said.

"What the fuck is this about? I look out for everybody. I even looked out for you a time or two."

"Nigga, this a robbery, not a question-asking interview. Now give me the blow you got. I know you got that work. And give me whatever money and stamps you got too."

"I don't have shit. I haven't picked up nothing yet. So whomever dropped the dime didn't get the timing right," Mo said.

Shorty 55 walked right up to Mo and snatched the chain off his neck.

"You going too far, 55. My grandbaby gave me that chain."

"Fuck you and your grandbaby. Give me what I came for."

"I told you I don't have it. I don't get shit 'til tonight when I pick up at pill-line. We can work something out then." Mo Garrett refused to show any signs of fear. And it wasn't an act; he really didn't have any. What will be will be.

"You see, I liked you, Mo Garrett. I liked you a lot. But you're playing with me. And I don't like to be played with. Why would you lose your life over some stupid bags of jailhouse blow? Think. I thought you were an old wise man."

Mo was a fighter. He'd been shot three times during three different robberies when he was younger. He just refused to negotiate with terrorists. He'd been like that his entire life.

"Look, son, you got the chain. And here, I got $20 for you that I had for a minute." Mo passed 55 the torn $20. He looked at it and smiled.

"That's *my* $20, you dumb muthafucka. That's the same $20 I gave one of my li'l men to come in here buy some dope from you a few minutes ago. You lying to me, OG. I sent my man in here to cop from you as soon as you took that work from your so-called sons. Your sons that gonna let you die in this bitch."

"You can't kill a ghost."

"Really? Well, I won't kill you then. I'll just torture your ass."

55 stepped back and nodded to his men. "Handle it."

Mo Garrett fought with everything in him as the knife went deep into his leg. They were aiming for his stomach, but Mo had skills and was able to deflect the first stabbing. But then all of those big, gorilla-looking men were on him. One of them got behind him and got Mo in a serious headlock. They were cutting off his air. Mo did not beg. He just fought. He was short of breath, and he felt himself about to black out. His feet were swinging back and forth.

"I think he might remember where he put the dope," 55 said.

The man holding Mo Garrett released his neck, and he took in a deep breath. 55 walked up in Mo's face and asked him again. Instead of Mo using his energy to tell where the work was, he hawked up a wad of spit and dumped it in Shorty 55's scarred up face.

"Fuhhh . . . you!" Mo managed to say.

"I gotta give it to him, he's definitely a fighter. Let's see how much he fights this hard dick in his ass."

Shorty 55 dropped his pants and took out his dick. He began massaging it until it was rock hard. "Pull his pants down so I can run up in that hairy ass."

Mo immediately came to his senses. He wasn't about to lose his manhood over blow. Now this was going *too* far.

"A'ight, look. Look under the sheet. The blow is there. Just take it and get the fuck out." Shorty 55's men grabbed the sheet, and lo and behold, there were the bags of cocaine.

"Bingo! I just hit dope heaven."

Mo was relieved. He'd rather die than get hit in the ass. "Hem his ass up again."

"What the fuck? You got what you wanted. Just get out of here," Mo said.

"Nah, I gotta teach your man Nasty a lesson. Him and Soulja think they got clout over a real boss, but I'ma show them how to respect rank. He'll think twice about saying fuck 55 again."

55's men pulled out two bottles of baby oil and squirted it all over Mo Garrett's cell. Then they hog-tied him and stuffed his mouth with a washcloth and tied it up. They put him in his bed before setting the cell on fire. After jamming his cell door, they ran out of there. Mo's screams went unheard, and all of the other men on the tier minded their own business. They knew exactly who was under those bandannas. They could cover their faces, but they could never change their walk or their voices.

Soon, the tier began to smell like smoke. Then the smoke alarm went off and correction officers were all over the place. They tried to open up Mo's cell, but it was jammed. While they were trying to get the door open, Mo Garrett sat in his bed burning alive . The last thing Mo Garrett heard before everything went black was, "This nigger's toast!"

CHAPTER 14

Tony was constantly blowing up Paige's phone, but she refused to answer. When it rang six times and went to voice mail, he tossed the phone across the room. He was pissed because he knew he was being purposely ignored. He wanted to see his daughter, and he was getting angrier and angrier that Paige was keeping Tonaya from him.

Paige contemplated answering his calls yesterday, but she did a drive-by to Sharise's place and saw that his car was still there. Crushed that he wasn't fighting harder for his family, Paige made her mind up that she was really and truly done with him. He went too far with Sharise . . . Spending the night over there. Openly parking his car in the driveway. He was being extremely disrespectful. She felt as if he was saying, "So what if Paige knows what I'm doing? It is what it is." The situation had gotten out of control in her mind, and she tried to force her heart to let Tony go.

Paige decided to go out and have a drink to clear her mind. She left the house alone. She didn't bother her girls to come with her. They would always watch Tonaya if necessary. They've always had each other's backs. When she walked into the Truth-Be-Told Lounge, she went straight to the bar. Not expecting to see anyone special, she didn't take the extra time to get dressed up. She had on a simple pair of blue stretch jeans, a baby tee, and knee-high black rider boots. She sipped on her Sex on the Beach, and that's when she suddenly spotted Mad-Dog. He was sitting at the table across from the bar with a girl. A beautiful, stunning girl at that. She immediately regretted coming out, and even more so, how she looked. She waved over the bartender and quietly paid for her drink. She cancelled her order of wings. All she could think about was getting the hell up out of there.

"Shit!" she said out loud to herself. He was seated in such a way that he faced the door. There was no way to make it out of there without being seen unless she walked extremely fast and didn't hesitate. She waited until he was deep in conversation with the mystery chick, and that's when she made her move. She got up, praying not to be noticed, but it was too late.

"Ay, yo, Paige!" Mad-Dog said, calling out to her. She stopped in her tracks and spun on her heels. A fake smile found its way to her face. She watched him as he left some money on the table and got up.

"Are you coming back?" the girl he was with said with a screwed up face.

"Nah. Have a good night, baby!"

She stood up in silent protest and put her hand on hip. He turned around and raised an eyebrow. The girl got the message and finally left. Just like that. Mad-Dog was very attractive. Everything from the way he walked . . . the way he bit his bottom lip sometimes when he smiled. He exuded control. Mad-Dog didn't look back once he saw the girl headed for the door. He was completely focused on Paige.

"Don't you have a date?" she said to him.

"Nah, I was just killing time until I ran into you or you called me back," he said. Paige was flattered. "You're even prettier under your makeup. For real, you don't even need to wear none," he said touching her cheek. "Can I kick it with you for a little while?"

"I really have to get back home to my baby."

"You just walked in here. You're not fooling nobody, Paige. Relax. Let's just chill for a minute."

Chill they did. And that went on for a while, starting something special. Every day Mad-Dog was either taking Paige out, buying her something, talking to her on the phone, or taking her out to eat. Something different each day. And each time was better than the last. He did not try to come at her sexually; he was being a real good friend, and he had a different energy than her girlfriends at home. He brought that masculine swag into her life, and she adored every second of it. So when he finally invited her over to his place to swim in his pool, she was more than willing.

"Mad-Dog, I gotta be real with you; you're a good man. You've been wining and dining me, and I definitely would love to be more than your friend. But your lifestyle is too much for me. I'm already worrying about you at night, and we're not even together," Paige said as she and Mad-Dog stood in front of each other. They were enjoying the warm night air in his pool. They'd been sipping Cîroc and Ace of Spades all night. They were both tipsy.

His arms were wrapped around Paige's waist, and his face was buried in her neck. "This is all I know, Paige. I'm not new at this. I've taken many precautions, so you have nothing to worry about. You gotta accept me as I am. If you can do that, I can cut down my list of females to just one."

The two of them had been spending a lot of time together, and they were both feeling the intense, rapid growth of feelings for each other. It was undeniable. He took Paige shopping a few times and laced both her and her daughter on several occasions. He was the perfect gentleman, and Paige was falling for him.

"You think you can really be with one woman? Are you convinced of that?" Paige asked.

"I've been convinced, ma. The real question is, how sure can I be that you're not still holding onto Tony? I mean, y'all got almost 10 years in, and I've never had a serious relationship before."

"Don't get me wrong, I still love Tony. I'd be lying if I said didn't. But I also know I gotta let him go. He forgot where his loyalty was supposed to be and turned his back on his family."

"Why do you think he turned his back on you? You told me what happened, but you haven't even spoke to dude."

"There is nothing to talk about. And to be honest, that shit was weak, and I cannot be with a man as weak as Tony."

"And now you're feeling me, huh?" he asked talking into her ear.

"Yes."

"You wanna know what I think? I think your heart is broken, and I'm just the guy that's been here to keep you company."

"In some ways that's true, Maddie. But I'm really liking you now. A lot," she said. She then turned to face him and kissed him for the first time.

"We can stay friends, Paige, until you're ready. I don't wanna push you into something, and then find out later that it is not what I thought it was."

"Shhh!" Paige said, putting her finger to her lips. "That's my song right there." The song "Take My Time" came on by Chris Brown. Paige began dancing sensually while she was in Maddie's arms.

"Baby, you gon' make a nicca wife you up for real. That's the only thing I'm missing in my life, for real."

"So don't talk about it; be about it."

He smiled. "You are something else."

"I try to be. Oh, and I told my big brother about you. Well, he's not my blood brother, but has always been like one to me. Soulja."

"And what did he say? I value his opinion. That's a real thoroughbred, right there. I bet he think I got a thousand females and wouldn't be no good for you."

"Actually, he said the opposite. He said you're a real man, and if I was serious about leaving Tony, that you would be a good man to be in me and my daughter's life. He said to tell you whattup."

"That's love. I'm glad he feels that way. Tell him I said keep his head up."

"You glad he feels that way, huh? Well, what about how *I'm* feeling?" Paige asked seductively. Maddie looked at the beautiful, yet vulnerable woman in front of him. He wasn't sure how to move, but his emotions got the best of him. He leaned in and kissed her. Passionately. He could feel that she was hungry for more of him.

Paige jumped up and wrapped her legs around Mad-Dog's waist. And the kiss continued. Long and passionate.

"Do you want me, Maddie?" she asked.

"Just as bad as you want me," he said. He could feel his hardness advancing in the direction of her vagina.

"How you know I want you so bad?" she asked.

"Because I can feel your body trembling, baby. And you're breathing heavy. And your nipples feel like marbles," he said, touching them ever so gently.

"Well, since you know so much, why am I out here with you and *not* in your bed?"

CHAPTER 15

The pen had been on lockdown for 2 weeks. Nasty paced in his cell back and forth like a caged lion. His heart was turning to ice as he dealt with two horrible blows. First, he heard that they were separating him and Soulja. The threat of retaliation for what happened to Mo Garrett was just too high. The staff didn't feel like dealing with a bloodbath, so they transferred Soulja. It was easier to transfer him since he had life. His new home would be the infamous Louisiana prison, "Blood" Pollock USP. Nasty, on the other hand, would stay right where he was at the Baltimore "Supermax" USP. Nasty hadn't been out of his cell; he had barely eaten and was living off of pure adrenaline. All he could think about was getting to Shorty 55. The warrior in him had been awakened, and somebody was going to pay a very hefty price.

He constantly thought about it. The smell of the smoke that day when Mo Garrett had been killed and him wondering what clown was causing a ruckus . . . He and Soulja were kicking it, doing nothing, while their man was totally vulnerable. He tried to tell himself it wasn't his fault, but he didn't believe that. When Mo Garrett asked to handle the situation, he could have stopped him, but he let Mo get involved. It wasn't Mo's beef. This was foul from every angle of foulness.

By the time the police went running to Mo's cell, it was too late. He'd heard the worst possible news. Mo Garrett had been tied up and burned to death. Defenseless. Not only did they kill Mo like an animal, but they snatched the chain from his neck that had a small locket with his granddaughter's picture inside. The young girl had leukemia and the necklace was precious to Mo. He was always kissing it after he finished his Islamic prayers. This was the ultimate violation. It took another day and a half before the lockdown was lifted, and Nasty was ready to set off World War III.

He badly wanted to talk with Soulja, but he was already gone, in the process of being transferred. Nasty went straight to the showers, and four of his men looked out while he washed. It had been days since he was able to properly clean himself. A sadness hung in the prison air like a low, thick fog. Everybody loved Mo Garrett, and even though he tried to front like he wasn't involved, everybody also knew that Shorty 55 was the one who orchestrated the hit.

"Yo, Nasty, how you plan on breaking even with them cats?" Rocky asked. "I feel guilty as fuck. But them niggas held a knife to my throat. There was nothing I could do."

"Don't blame yourself. Nobody expected Shorty 55 to get down like this," Nasty said.

"So what's the next move?" Rocky questioned.

"I'm not sure yet, but somebody's blood gon' pour like a waterfall—even if it has to be mine."

"You already know them niggas is anticipating our move, so we might as well vest up and get busy as soon as them doors open to the other side. Plus, it's a couple of them on this block that we can hit right now," Rocky said. Nasty couldn't help but to think about Soulja and what he would say. They had often played vicious chess matches, and one thing Nasty knew was how to strategize an attack. He'd been beat enough times by Soulja that he learned to almost anticipate moves like a psychic. He knew this. He was trained, so he had to fight against his bloodthirst to remain still for the time being. Planning was important.

His two confidants, Soulja and Mo Garrett, were both gone. The only person to make decisions now was him. And he had to admit, he wasn't sure what to do. He didn't want to react off of pure emotion. That's when most mistakes were made. He needed to clear his mind and get his thoughts together.

"You're right, Rock, they're waiting on us. We can't just react. Let me plan the assault." Nasty and Rocky dapped on it. They both stayed vested up in case Shorty 55 was really looking for all-out war. And Nasty ordered men to stand outside his cell around the clock. Nasty sent for the correction officer who was holding his cell phone for him to slide it over to him through his meal hole so he could hold it down for a couple of days. He had business. He sent word for Soulja to call him once he got to Louisiana. Two days later, his phone vibrated; the number said unavailable.

"What's up, baby boy? You all right, fam?" Soulja asked.

"Nah, I'm not. We were doing fine up until 2 weeks ago."

"I know, fam, I know," Soulja said. "But you're not gonna like what I have to say."

"And what's that, brother?"

"We can't go back down that old road that trapped us in the gates of hell. Let it go."

Nasty took the phone from ear and looked at it. He thought he was hearing things. "Fuck you mean let it go?"

"I just found out that we got access to over 30 duplexes, dirt cheap. That's 60 apartments, yo. Our shit is coming together nicely. For less than $50,000, all them cribs are ours. We can do what we want with them. You know how dope that is? We can really impact the city. Fix 'em up, rent 'em out for $500 to $800 a whop and Section 8 'em for like $1,500. Bro, that's about $40,000 to $50,000 a month right there. Legit. It ain't dope money, but nobody can take it from us."

"How you even thinking about that shit at a time like this?"

"'Cause that's what Mo would want us to do."

"Pops would have died for us if something like that happened to one of us. I'm not 'bout to sit around like some square-headed muthafucka and let them get away with fuckin' over Mo like that. Hell, no!"

"So you're just willing to say fuck our plans? Fuck freedom? Fuck everything that we worked hard with Mo to build? You're too smart for that," Soulja schooled. "We've got shit to do much bigger than jailhouse antics. Don't get me wrong, what happened to Mo is foul, but we can honor him properly. As a matter of fact, I thought about naming the spot Mo Garrett Housing. What better way to honor him? I even got Keva setting up a corporation for us. Come on, man. I'm depending on you. Without you, this is all for not. I'm not getting out . . . ever. So why throw it all away? Just fall back and get out of there."

"I can't lie, the plan sounds good. It does. But I can't live with myself if I just let this go. This shit is war. War was brought to my front door, and a nicca like me gotta settle the score, baby."

"Yo, the struggle is a dangerous thing. We win some, and we lose some. But you still have your life. Mo wasn't never leaving the joint. But you are. It's time you prioritize yourself," Soulja advised.

"Listen, you talkin' something right now that I can't

really process. My mind ain't there right now. I'm not focused."

Soulja was happy that he got shipped. Had he been there, today would have set off the prison version of Vietnam. He would have fed off of Nasty's energy, and the two of them would have created havoc. Now he had to convince his man to calm down. He knew it wouldn't be easy, but he had to try.

"I'm not trying to lose you, Nasty. Point-blank. It's not worth it. There's a whole new world out there for you. We have plans. And remember what Mo Garrett said. He told us that no matter what happens, we *have* to do this. We have to be soldiers of change. He told us to take our hustling minds into the business world."

"How are you so calm?"

"I'm not calm. I'm focused," Soulja responded.

"We can't look soft, dog. We can't let niccas think they can hit somebody that close to us and nothing happen."

Soulja knew this was true, but in reality, he was being a little bit selfish. He loved Nasty like a true brother and didn't want to risk losing him. But he understood that in war, sometimes, there were casualties. He just wasn't prepared for one of those casualties to be Nasty.

"Understood. Okay, look. Everybody off lock, right?"

"Yeah," Nasty said.

"Okay, I'ma make our stance real clear. Give me a

couple of days. And I'ma be looking in your window! But in the meantime, stand down."

"So that's law?" Nasty asked.

"That's law. One, love."

"One, love." Nasty hung up the phone pissed. He was mad that he couldn't put work in right now. But he never went against Soulja, so he had to wait . . . even though it killed him.

Nasty called a meeting on the yard. There were 10 of them, and they met at the picnic tables at the far west end of the compound.

"So what's the word?" Bam asked, a loyal soldier of theirs.

"Soulja said to lay back and lay low for a minute until we see it necessary to move."

Bam jumped to his feet. "Man, what? Yo ain't even here, so how he gonna advise us what to do? No disrespect, Soulja gone, so we gotta do what's best for us. Ain't no soft-ass shit over here."

"I'ma let your comment slide because we're all upset right now. But what Soulja says is law. So we're gonna chill until I advise otherwise."

"You're not worried about these punks thinking we

went soft?" Rocky asked.

"It will actually create the opposite. They think we're gonna strike, and when we don't, it will throw them off their square. Soulja knows what he's talking about."

Really, Nasty didn't want to tell his crew that Soulja wanted to let things go overall. They would never understand that; shit . . . he barely understood it himself. But he trusted Soulja, and he knew that he would never let them go out like suckers. Something would be done. He would give Soulja a couple of weeks, and then if he heard nothing else, he would make his own decisions.

CHAPTER 16

"Just like that, baby. Just like that!" The sound of Sharise's humming vibrated on Tony's dick. It had him at full attention. She was a professional head giver. She had some type of spell with that shit. He couldn't help himself. At night when she begged him to slob his tool, he let her. And he exploded in her mouth on a regular basis. She loved that shit. She sat up and wiped her mouth, then lay down beside him.

"Gottdamn, Sharise," Tony said. "I should be the one taking care of you right now after you hooked me up with that Colombian connect."

"Well, that's my job. He's real cool. I've been trying to get at him for years, but he would never fuck with me. But he peeped how you've been moving and said he would give you a key of dope for $75,000."

"Yes, and that shit was a good look. Now I'm making real moves."

"Nah, now WE are making real moves," Sharise corrected. She wanted to make it clear to Tony that they were a team. She wanted to attach herself to him in every way possible. She saw the potential in Tony firsthand, and she wasn't about to miss out on the mega come up.

That $75,000 he spent on that key of dope was almost all that Tony had, but he made a wise investment and copped it. It was more than worth it. The money he made after flipping that kilogram really put him on the map. Now he was able to buy three more keys and things were coming together perfectly. Shit was moving, and Tony was moving on up. He was breaking those keys down quickly and killing the streets. His street soldiers respected him; he paid them more than their fair share. He was on point and surpassed many of dealers who were getting shit that had been stomped on two or three times. He was dealing with a straight Colombian connect. And everybody knew, the best suppliers were Africans and Colombians. With his own connect, Tony was about to rise straight to the top. He learned how to stretch the key. Not too much as to where the high wasn't good but enough to make a good flip on his money. He was still faithful; the quality of heroin needed to make a fiend happy. And happy they were.

Sharise was ghetto smart. He did respect her in that regard. She knew how to flip a social service check into a few thousand dollars' worth of coke and bring every penny of it back to the bank. They worked well together, and he was beginning to trust her and let his heart open up to her a li'l bit more. She had a good eye and could convince most people of anything. Tony was feeling her in that aspect. Her hustle mentality was attractive, but he didn't feel for her the way she felt for him. Sharise was now in love with Tony, without a doubt. Her self-motivated reasons for using him had transformed into something else. She was deeply into him, and Tony had never had a woman openly worship him the way she did. But his heart was still with Paige.

He had never told Sharise he loved her. Whenever she told him, he just flipped the conversation and praised her for whatever she did that day. Sharise was no fool, and she knew Tony was still loving Paige. But she knew how to take care of that. She planned to up her game. She wanted Tony all to herself, and all she needed was a little bit more time to make that happen.

Tony recently copped a new silver Range Rover. He rocked a few nice pieces of jewelry too and was ready to let Paige see what he was working with. He wanted her to see that he could take care of her and Tonaya like never before and that Mad-Dog was no competition.

Sharise went to the shower. She came out drying her hair with her robe open, exposing her nakedness to Tony. "Baby, a friend of mine has a car for sale. It's almost new. It's a BMW 6 Series. It's really nice. I think I would look nice in it."

"I think you would look nice in it too."

She smiled when he said that.

"So start saving up for it," he said.

She frowned at that.

"I want you to buy it for me, baby. It's only $45,000. My friend's brother went on the run, and he's getting rid of it. Why can't you get it for me?"

"Sharise, why would I drop $45,000 on a car right now? That doesn't even make sense." Tony couldn't believe she asked him something like that when he hadn't even dropped anything on Tonaya and Paige yet. He only gave her $2,000 once when he first got started. He slid it under the door at the old house. But right now, Sharise was trippin'. "I don't have it like that."

"Yes, you do. You can use some of the money from the floor safe."

"Nah. That money is in case a storm hits, Sharise. Don't you remember your advice about bail and lawyers and even a possible ransom situation?" he argued.

"Yeah, but there's $180,000 in there now. And that doesn't include the other stash where I been putting extra money. I talked to them. They'll take $30,000 now and the other $15,000 in a month. He said he'll do it like that for you because he sees how smooth you move, and he knows you're good for it. He said he knows you're good for it tenfold." Sharise was exaggerating, stroking Tony's ego, knowing how badly he wanted to be recognized for his hustle game. That was all it took.

"I been thinking about putting you in something, Sharise, but that 650i might be a little bit much to start."

"But, Tone, you're pushing a fat-ass Range. Bitches is already about to be swinging from your nuts—including Paige. And let me remind you that she's already shitting on you, rolling around with Mad-Dog. Everybody knows they're together. It's not a secret. But don't worry; once she sees how you're flossing and that your girl is pushing that new Beema, she's going to be sick."

Tony did not like the idea of hurting Paige, but he didn't like how Paige was disrespecting him with Mad-Dog.

"So what's up, Tony?"

"I don't know, Sharise."

"Well, I can give you another reason to make sure I'm riding well. And safe."

"And what is that?"

"I'm pregnant. I found out yesterday."

Tony thought he was hearing things. "Come again?" he said.

"'Yes, Tony. I'm pregnant with *your* baby. Aren't you happy for us?" she asked. Tony felt his world instantly start to crumble. He'd be lying if he said he had no love for Sharise, but his love for Paige was a million times more. He did not want to hurt Paige like that. But then he questioned why he cared so much when Paige had so easily moved on with the next nicca. His head was all over the place.

Sharise smiled to herself. She was lying about the

pregnancy. She only said it to see his reaction, and the next words out of her mouth were supposed to be just that . . . that she was only joking around. But she had a change of heart.

"Sharise, I'm not ready for another child. And my mother is going to have a panic attack." Tony immediately thought about his mother's reaction. She was a church fanatic. He hated the idea of having to explain to her another child out of wedlock. It took forever for her to accept Paige and Tonaya. That was another thing . . . Paige. Great!

"It's all good, Tony. We have more than enough money now. And if you're worried about your parents, we can just get married next month. It's all good. See? Problem solved."

"The car is enough for now. The baby has to wait."

"So you want me to get an abortion?"

"I think that's best. And I'll get with you later about the car."

Sharise got what she wanted. She wanted that car, but she also allowed Tony to think she really was pregnant. She figured she could get more out of him, even though it stung for a minute that he wanted her to get an abortion. But her mind was off of that and focused on how she would look riding around, flossin' in her new BMW. She had a statement to make.

"Okay. I'll make an appointment with the doctor. But

don't you want some of this pregnant pussy before you leave?" she asked. She dropped her robe and rubbed her hand up and down her crotch. Tony's manhood instantly reacted.

"I never turn down that down, baby." Tony was going to give it to Sharise real good. Anything at this point to keep her willing to get the abortion. He'd rather buy a BMW than a crib.

CHAPTER 17

Von looked around at her friends and smiled inside her heart. She felt that she was so blessed with the best group of women she could possibly have. They were a family in their own right. They all loved each other and would do anything to help her get through this horrible time in her life. Von wasn't too big on going out. With her being pregnant and all, most nights, her girls brought the entertainment to her.

"Girl, we set their ass. I told you we should have bid 10. You know I'm the Spades queen," Marla said as she slapped hands with Von. Paige and their other friend Tina were done. They lost $500 already and didn't want to lose any more.

"Whatever. Y'all bitches got lucky," Paige said as she sipped on some Hennessy. Paige had never been into drinking, but she was sippin' and feeling nice. Everybody could see how happy she was now that she had Mad-Dog in her world.

"So what's been going on with you and Maddie?" Von

asked Paige. She got up from the card table to grab some water and swallow a few pills.

"We've been chilling."

"Chillin' as in fucking? Have you given it up yet?" Marla asked.

"That ain't none of your business," Paige said. And then she coughed.

"That cough always gives it away. Yeah, bitch, you gave it up. Was it good?"

"You know what . . . y'all crazy," Paige responded.

"Just tell us. Stop acting brand new," Marla said.

"Okay, okay. Yeah. It went down."

"Whaaat? You lying!" Marla said.

"I hope you used protection."

"We did," Paige answered. Lying.

"You better."

Paige made a mental note to make Mad-Dog strap up next time.

"But the good news is, we are official. I'm his girl, and he's my man. We decided to take it to the next level."

"That's great, Paige. I'm happy for you," Marla said.

"I'm happy too, but don't you think you need a little bit more time before you jump into another relationship? I mean, I know how much you love Tony."

"Girl, fuck Tony. I'm still high from the way Mad-Dog

made love to me. He took his time. It was so sensual and passionate."

"Tony would blow a fuse if he knew you were being sexed by someone else. Girl, this is gonna be bad."

"What's bad is the way I'm falling for Maddie. He is so sexy. Girl, if you could have been a fly on that wall to see how he handled this . . ."

"Paige, enough about your sex life. Let me tell y'all this shit," Marla said as Paige fanned herself. "I went to see your brother, Von. His ass is so damn fine, it should be illegal."

"Girl, I do not wanna hear about my brother being fine," Von said, shaking her head.

"Well, anyway, when I got there, Rodney's ass was there."

"Rodney? What the hell was *he* doing there? Was this before or after I told him he was sick?"

"Before. I just forget to tell y'all. Well, honey, I wasn't supposed to be there. I just showed up. But Rodney's funky ass happened to be summoned by Nasty."

"So what happened?" Paige questioned.

"Well, he dismissed me, talkin' 'bout they had to have a meeting. He sent me in the li'l kids' room to watch *Sesame Street*." Paige and Von busted out laughing. "But that didn't mean shit. You know I'm a professional lip reader. Basically, from what I could see, Nasty gave him his walking papers. And checked him for mistreating you."

"He did? I thought he wanted me to get back with him."

"Come on now, girl. You know Nasty don't play that shit when it comes to you."

Von smiled, knowing that her brother was still his old self, coming to her defense.

"That's good. Maybe he'll listen to Nasty and stay away from me until the baby comes. I don't want him nowhere near me."

"I feel you," Paige said. Suddenly, Marla's cell phone rang. She got up to take the call. She came back in 10 minutes and sat down with a confused look on her face.

"Okay, well, that was one of my gossiping-ass friends from work. I had her check on a few things before I shared it with y'all. You are not going to believe this," Marla said.

"Believe what?" Von asked.

"Yeah, tell," Paige said.

"Have y'all heard about Tony?" Marla said.

"What about him? Did something happen?" Paige asked, concerned. When she noticed how everyone saw how worried she got, she quickly checked herself and screwed up her face.

"Nah, nothing happened to him, but his name is starting to ring bells."

"Ring bells? Girl, ringing bells about what? You know Tony is always at work. Actually, he had two jobs, last I knew. So what is his name ringing bells about?"

"Girl, Tony is deep in the game!"

"What are you talking about, Marla?"

"I'm telling you, Tony is out there slinging dope with the best of 'em."

Paige couldn't believe her ears. That didn't make any sense.

"I wasn't going to say anything until I confirmed the information, but I now know that Tony is driving a new Range Rover, and that bat Sharise is pushing a 650 BMW. Word is, he got it for her."

The anger that surged through Paige turned her skin a bright red. She got up from her seat and began to pace. "Are you sure about this, Marla?"

"One hundred percent, baby."

"I can't believe this muthafucka. He out there buying cars and trucks, but all he gave me and Tonaya was $2,000 a few weeks ago. He got a lot of nerve. I can't believe he's doing all this for that bitch. This ain't right." Tears began to build up in her eyes. This pain was different than the pain she felt when she found out Tony was cheating. She thought maybe he just got caught up, doing what men do from time to time. But it looked like he was really serious about this bitch, and *that* burnt her up.

"It's okay, Paige. You got Mad-Dog now," Marla said.

"That's not the point. And to think, he just texted me

about bringing Tonaya to him. I was going to do it. But fuck that. He don't need to be around my daughter. As a matter of fact, I'ma file child support on his ass. I'll be handling that first thing Monday."

"I don't blame you," Marla added. "And I wouldn't let my daughter be around that shit either. Sometimes you gotta hit these niggas where it hurts."

"And what he know about the game? He's a damn joke. Tony don't know nothing about getting no damn street money."

"Well, that's not what the streets are saying."

Paige was steaming. "It's all good. He won't be around my baby while he's out there experimenting."

"What is wrong with y'all? You're trippin'. You can't keep that man from his child. That's not right. You know how much Tonaya loves her father."

"I'm not even trying to hear none of that right now. His ass is on ice, plain and simple. Fuck Tony's sorry ass. I can raise Tonaya all by myself. And shit, Mad-Dog might be an even better father anyway."

Von just shook her head. She knew that Paige was hurt and was talking from a place of pain. But it was dead wrong to keep a father away from his child and to have another man playing his role.

All Paige could think about is all the years she and Tony spent together. She wanted to literally kill him herself for doing this. But rather than act out her thoughts, she excused herself from the ladies and went in the bathroom to call her man.

"Maddie, can you come pick me up? I'm missing you like crazy!" Fuck it, the only cure for an old man is a new one.

CHAPTER 18

"Keva, how are you and my baby doing?" Soulja asked.

"We're good. What about you? How is this new prison?"

"It's the same. All this shit is the same. Don't worry about me, baby . . . How are you?"

"I'm fine. And this li'l girl of yours thinks she's grown." Keva then whispered, "Soulja, she's looking more and more like her mother, Teja. I don't think we'll be able to keep the truth from her for long. In a couple of years, she'll want to know. She's the smartest li'l kid I've ever seen."

"We'll cross that bridge when we get there. And why you say she's grown?"

"Because this girl ain't been in kindergarten but for 2 weeks, and she's already suspended for 6 days."

"What? What the hell happened?" he asked.

"She was raising her hand in class. And she said the teacher kept ignoring her. So she stood up and told him that if he ignored her one more time, she was going to have him killed." Soulja could not contain himself. He laughed so hard, he had to put the phone down and wipe his eyes. His li'l girl was crazy just like him.

"You lying, yo!" he said still laughing.

"That shit ain't funny. The girl is only 5 years old," Keva said.

"Okay, okay. Put her li'l ass on the phone." Soulja could hear her come running once Keva called out to her.

"Hi, Daddy," she said out of breath.

"Hi, baby. What you doing, I'sa?"

"I was making my Barbie dolls karate fight." Soulja had to really contain himself because he wanted to laugh again. But he didn't want her to think it was okay to be so violent. "Oh, and I was doing the Dab in the mirror."

"My baby can dance, huh?"

"Yup. I'll show you how I do it on the next visit."

"Well, before we get into all that, let's talk about why you got suspended at school."

"He picks on me, Daddy. He is always giving me funny looks. But Mommy doesn't believe me." He could hear Keva chastising her in the background.

"Don't be stressing out your father with your storytelling, I'sa."

"But I am for real. He acts funny toward me."

Soulja hated going against anything that Keva laid down as far as disciplining I'sa. "I'sa, what did I tell you about listening to your mother? You have to be a good girl. Just because the teacher didn't do something you want doesn't give you the right to threaten his life."

"But, Daddy, I do listen to Mommy. But it hurts my feelings when Mommy believes somebody over me. You told me that family comes first, and if somebody disrespects me, that you would threaten their life. So I just did it myself since you not here with me." Soulja could not believe that this li'l girl remembered all that. She was the female version of him, and he felt proud as hell.

All Keva could do was shake her head as she thought to herself, *Like father like daughter.*

And he thought about what Keva said. Yes, she was too smart to be lied to. One day he would have to come clean. Soulja was slowly preparing his mind for having to tell li'l I'sa the truth one day about her mother:

Soulja and Nasty were in Brazil. He was in love with Teja like never before. She was a beautiful Brazilian woman with dark features and a goddesslike presence. Her beauty could pierce any man's soul. She was the daughter of one of Nasty's parents' connects. They fell in love as little kids when Soulja saw her across the street playing in the yard with Paige. He went and kicked his li'l 14-year-old game, and she bought it. They thought nothing would ever separate them. Then, Nasty's parents were murdered.

Teja's parents were killed as well. She was stuck in the United States without any family, but she had money. More money than any 16-year-old girl should have or know what to do with. But she did. She got herself an apartment in Baltimore, and Soulja spent most of his nights there with her. This went on for years until Soulja had made it big time and copped a nice condo for them downtown Baltimore. He was living large. Many men twice his age hadn't accomplished what he had. He had the game in a choke hold. He was respected and feared.

One day, Teja came home with tears in her eyes.

"What's wrong, baby?" Soulja asked.

"I'm pregnant."

"Are you serious?" he asked feeling his stomach do flips.

"Yes. I am serious. I'm so happy I can't stop crying."

Soulja dropped to his knees and asked Teja to marry him. He was young, but he'd become a man long ago. And now he felt he needed a wife. With a family to love and protect, he felt he had it all. Teja was everything to him. He treated her like a queen. Then one day, it all changed.

Soulja woke up, and Teja was gone. It was the middle of the night. Her belly had gotten huge, and she was ready to deliver any day. There was no reason that a young, pregnant woman should be out at three in the morning. He ran downstairs to the building's underground garage. Her Mercedes was still there. He thought about all the precautions he had taken that had proved useless. Her car was bulletproof. The car had a tracking system, but that did him no good because it was right here. He should have known that though because she could barely fit behind the steering wheel and Soulja had to drive her everywhere. He called her phone, but it went to voice mail. Soulja panicked. He wasn't just worried about Teja, but his unborn child as well. This was not like her. He called Nasty, and he came straight over.

"Where do you think she could have gone? I don't like this," Nasty said as he loaded his semiautomatic handgun.

"If somebody hurt her, scared her, threatened her, Imam —"

"And I'm right with you, yo! You think somebody nabbed her for ransom?" Nasty asked, his voice laced with uncertainty.

"If so, I ain't heard shit. Nobody's asking for nothing. But you know I will run this city red for my baby. I can't think of an Imam crazy enough to fuck with mine," Soulja said. They waited a day, and then they would start running up in local hustlers' spots, demanding information. That was the best thing Soulja could think of. And then his phone rang. He answered and didn't say anything. The number was private.

"Soulja, baby, it's me. I know you're upset. But listen to

me, I'm in Brazil. "

"Brazil? Why?"

"I didn't want to say anything to you. But I know you are a man of honor," Teja said in her strong Brazilian accent. "I know who killed Nasty's parents, and before I have you come out here, I had to check my source. Yes, it's true. I know who did it." Soulja motioned for Nasty to stand near him. Then he put the phone on speaker.

"Are you sure?"

"Yes, I'm sure. Remember when they found her, her diamond ring was missing? Well, I found it. I checked it out myself. I know who it was. They run El Domino Cartel here. They have tens of millions of dollars' worth of cocaine and heroin. Come right away; I will have everything set up for you. You kill them, and we take the product. I have a way to get it back into the United States. Look in the drawer next to my side of the bed. That's how you can reach me when you get here. I love you. Me and your baby are safe. Come and get us." Then the line went dead.

Nasty was pacing the room. There was no calming him down. He'd dreamed about getting to the people who killed his parents. Soulja was in his own world because he was pissed she would do this. But her family came from the game, so it was in her blood.

"We got to go. I have to make sure my baby is safe," Soulja said.

"I've been waiting for the day I could avenge my

family."

Soulja and Nasty went to Brazil the very next morning. And nothing was what they expected. They'd been set up. And as hard as it was for Soulja to accept it, Teja was behind the whole thing.

"So, baby, are you going to be respectful at school?"

"I *am* respectful, Daddy. Why doesn't anybody believe me?"

"It's not that I don't believe you—"

"Well, if I told you the other things he said, you would be really mad. That's why I didn't say anything."

Keva looked at her with scorn. "You better be not be lying, li'l girl. What else did he say?"

"I don't want to tell Daddy."

Soulja could hear the stress in his daughter's voice. This concerned him. "What is it, baby? You can tell me anything, remember?"

"Okay. Well, Mr. Rosario said out loud in front of everybody to excuse my behavior because I don't have a dad. And I'm gonna end up in jail just like my father. He called me . . . umm, I don't remember how to say it . . . worf-less."

Soulja felt his eyes watering. He had changed his life's

purpose a little bit too late. He wanted to be there for her. His daughter was his sanity, and he could not fathom the thought of someone hurting her, not even her feelings. He was hurt and far beyond pissed off.

"It's okay, baby. You know that is not true, right?" he said. He noticed a tear had run down his cheek. He hated not being there.

"I know. But it was mean."

Now he understood why I'sa had gotten so upset. This teacher was a clown.

"Okay, baby, well, don't let anybody mess up what you know to be true. What is the poem I taught you?" he asked. "Let's say it together." Soulja had been saying this to her since she was a baby.

"Daddy is the King, and I'm his Princess.

We have a special bond and it's nobody's business.

I will do good in school so I can grow up and be rich.

I'll be strong, have honor, and never be a snitch.

And if anybody ever tries to cause me any harm

Daddy will come in the night and break both their arms."

She giggled.

"That's right, baby, 'cause I would give up my life for you in a heartbeat. I don't know if you know what that means, but I would. Okay?"

"Okay, Daddy. I love you."

"I love you too. Put Mommy on the phone."

Keva took the phone.

"This clown can't be serious," Soulja said.

"I'll be up there in the morning. I didn't know all that. I hope she's telling the truth."

"She got my blood, and we don't lie. Have you met this clown?"

"Well, actually, no. He's a new teacher. Her original teacher was killed in a car accident the third day of school. This man was a replacement. So I didn't meet him on parent-teacher night. I don't know anything about him."

"If he knows what I know, he better find another child to pick on!" Soulja hung up already pissed. He thought about how the peaceful approach didn't always work. And that fueled his next move. He made a phone call from his cell phone to his street soldier Moon.

"Whattup, Soulja," Moon said. "What's good?"

"Two things. Number one, I need you to put a car on my daughter's teacher. He knows I'm in prison, and I don't know how that's possible. Check homeboy out. His name is Rosario."

"On it. And what else?" Moon asked.

"This cat Shorty 55 that killed Mo Garrett? I need the whereabouts of all his children . I believe he has two sons and a daughter."

"Yeah. Now *that's* what I'm talking about. I'll keep you

posted."

"Once you've located him, call me on the cell." Soulja hung up the phone. He wanted to keep Nasty out of trouble, but he realized that one thing would have to always stand true: death before dishonor.

CHAPTER 19

Rodney cut open one of the three new keys of dope he just bought from a new supplier. He didn't like dealing with cartels because there was always too much red tape. But the price was good. $68,000 for a key of heroin was unheard of. He had to take the deal. He opened it and passed it to the fiend. He did his thing and in 5 minutes, the fiend was wrapping his arm with a rubber band and looking for a vein.

"Hurry up!" Rodney demanded.

"I'm trying to find a good spot. Just hold on. Hold on."

Rodney was getting impatient. He wanted to know if the shit was any good. Finally the fiend took off the rubber band. He stood up and dropped his pants.

"What the hell are you doing?" Rodney said.

"I need a good spot." The dope fiend shot the dope into his balls. Then he sat down on an old dirty mattress and waited for the drug to course his veins. He waited, and waited . . . and then his eyes closed. He opened them back up in a few seconds.

"This shit is lightweight."

"Lightweight? Be more specific."

"It's trash. I don't feel nothing, really," the dope fiend said. Rodney was pissed. He kicked the chair in front of him.

"A'ight, get up outta here," Rod said. The man left.

"Go see that Mexican piece of shit and tell him I want my money back," Rodney told his top lieutenant, Lucky. Lucky left after making a phone call to the Mexican. Rodney sat back in his chair and shook his head. He wasted over $200,000 on garbage. He could just charge it to the game, but he had too much pride. And he should have known better. The shit was just too cheap.

He picked up his phone and dialed Von's number. She answered.

"What do you want?" she said.

"How is my baby doing?"

"Your baby's health is in God's hands. I don't know. Did you start informing those girls you've been with that they need to be tested?"

"You're jumping the gun, Von. You are assuming that *I* got that shit. I just read that a man can pass it to a woman and never contract it. I don't think I got it."

"What do you mean you don't think? Are you stupid, Rod? Do you want to die?"

"Listen, tell me when you're going to the doctor next. I

wanna see the sonogram of the baby."

"Not until you tell those girls. Rodney, that's evil. You better start talking, or I will." Then she hung up on him.

He stared at the phone in disgust. She was trying to put that dirty disease on him. Shit, for all he knew, Von could have fucked somebody else and got it. He wasn't with her all the time. Other possibilities started running through his mind. With each possibility, he became more and more convinced that he did not transmit the disease. He desperately wanted to believe that Von was running game on him because she was upset that he had been cheating. He didn't want to believe that he having the disease was even possible. So he slowly but surely convinced himself that it was a lie. If it was true, the shit would have to pop up from behind a bush one day and karate chop his immune system. That is the only way he would accept that he had the disease. The truth would have to literally smack him in the face.

Rodney was disturbed from his reverie when his boy Lucky came back through the door an hour later. He didn't look like he was bringing any news that Rodney wanted to hear.

"He said he not gonna take back the dope."

"Fuck you mean this bean-eating muh'fucka won't take back the work?" Rodney asked.

"He said he gave you the same quality that he sells everybody else, and nobody else complains. And he won't take it back."

"This shit is weak. Stepped on too many times. The Nigerians are coming way more correct."

"Rod, he said you need to holla at him yourself. He won't deal with me."

"Oh, I intend to holla at him, and if this dick sucker try to play me, I'ma rob his ass after I kill him and his bodyguard. Fuck them spics. I'd prefer to deal with the Africans anyway."

"Yeah, but you gotta watch them Nigerians. They start snitching immediately once they get grabbed by the law."

"You're right. I don't trust them spics or them goat-eating Africans," Rodney said with insults spraying from his tongue.

"Oh, Rod, I needed to tell you something. Man, this is gonna have you upset, but I figured you needed to know. I wouldn't be your man if I didn't put you on."

"What?" he asked, frowning up his face. He did not like the sound of Lucky's voice.

"I was at the store with my girl and across the street is that AIDS clinic. I saw Von coming out of there. You know her and my girl is cool, so she went over and talked to her for a minute. I waited. When she got back in the car she told me that Von had a paper in her hand that talked about how to manage your disease. I don't think she intended for my girl to see it. But she did. Is she doing some type of volunteer work or something?"

"Nah. She claim she got that shit."

"What? Man, that's fucked up, Rod. I hope that's not true. I ain't trying to lose one of my brothers like that," Lucky said.

"I'm good. I don't have that shit."

"Oh? So you got tested?" Lucky asked.

"Nah, I just know. My body is too strong for that. I know myself. I'm cool as a spring breeze," he said.

"Man, fuck that. You better go get tested and take that good medicine while it's still HIV. They've got new drugs now. At least you can live a normal life, fam," Lucky suggested.

Lucky couldn't help but to think about all the unprotected sex he'd had over the years. And the couple of trains he ran on hoes messing with Rodney. All *he* could think about was going to get tested.

Rod quickly changed the subject. "Look, fuck all that. We need to put some dope on the block right there. Tony cleaning up shop. The shit was dead; now it's jumping."

"Yeah, Rod, but Tony got it jumping. Let him eat. You told him it was all good. That would be foul to move him, and you gave him the green light."

"Well, I wanna get some of that rush while it's good. Tony was the guinea pig to see if this block was worth my time. Turns out it is. And I'ma set up shop."

"You're a cold dude, Rodney."

"That's how you get to the top. This dope is getting sold over here one way or another. And if Tony got a problem with that, he can pack up his shit and move to another spot. I made that strip, not Tony. Fuck him and that freak bitch Sharise."

CHAPTER 20

Moon pulled up to the corner of Eager Street in an all-black and dark-tinted Yukon Denali. Two stolen vans followed him. Both driven by other men who were loyal to both Nasty and Soulja. All of the men were dressed in black Tims, black sweat suits, and black knitted caps. The six men were nothing to play with. All of them had put in plenty of work and were always ready for war. Moon got out of his truck and walked up to the other trucks which were sitting side by side. Then he walked between them.

"Tee, you get out. Watch both corners. The rest of y'all sit tight and wait for my signal."

Cars were going up and down the two-lane street, not paying them any mind. A few locals were across the street. A man bouncing a basketball. A dog barking, and two older cats drinking Colt 45 malt liquor out of large cans, half-concealed in rumpled up brown paper bags. A typical Baltimore scene on a typical Baltimore day.

They pulled up on the side of the federal holding facility in Baltimore. It was a vulnerable place. They were on the side of the building where prisoners could see the streets. The old window above on C-Block that was only about 8 inches wide had an infamous crack in it. It had been that way for years. People from the street would call out to inmates all the time. It was just something to do. But tonight, that crack would serve a real purpose.

"Ay, yo," Moon called out from his truck with the window half open. "Somebody get Shorty 55 for me."

A random inmate had gone to get Shorty 55. But the way the windows were set, the inmates could see out and the people outside could not see in. All they saw were shadows. It was the yelling that allowed communication to happen.

The prison was back in full swing. Everybody was confused because even the guards had expected some kickback over Mo Garrett, but everybody was jive fucked up that nothing happened. People were starting to wonder if Nasty had gone soft since Mo and Soulja were gone. The only thing that had gotten around was that Nasty sent word to Shorty 55 asking for Mo Garrett's chain.

Sitting in his cell all alone, Nasty felt like he would explode from all the pressure. Everyone had expectations of him, but he was trying his best to be loyal to Soulja's wishes, even though it was killing him, and he felt people were questioning his gangster. Every time someone came back and told him what was being said in the penitentiary streets, it felt like a sledgehammer was banging against his skull. He wouldn't be able to hold back for much longer.

His boy Rocky came into his cell. "Listen, shit not looking good right now, fam. Them two niccas that came in here yesterday and copped from you didn't pay. They got it on some I-owe-you shit, but them two always pay. They testing you, Nasty. We gotta let it be known that we not playing with these cats."

Nasty shrugged Rocky's words off as though he didn't care. But he did. "They'll pay. They've never let me down before, so why would I overreact now? You're paranoid."

"I'm telling you . . . People think we went soft or some shit. They killed a man who was practically like your father, and we didn't do shit. I understand your reason for delay, but we gotta act now. I mean, come on. This is going against honor. The hell with what Soulja's talkin' 'bout. "

"Watch it!" Nasty said pointing at Rock. He valued Rocky's opinion, but there was still rank that needed to be respected. Rocky just shook his head and walked out. Frustrated. Everybody was frustrated. Nasty stood in his doorway and observed the prison. From his cell, which was on the third floor in the middle of the tier, he could see most of the movement around the prison.

For most of the prison's 2,000 residents, looking out that old window onto Eager Street was the biggest piece of freedom many of them would get for at least a decade. Some, for the rest of their lives. That window, with its old beat-up-looking frame and rusty bars, was the most beautiful sight to so many of them. You could hear the cars honking, emergency sirens, shouting, laughing, crying, and if you were important enough, maybe even someone calling your name.

"Yo, tell 55 he got a social at the window," Nasty heard someone say. He perked up, wondering who was calling his enemy. The window could only be looked out from the east side of the prison from the auditorium. The "Freedom Window" as they called it. Just like that, Rocky was back at Nasty's cell.

"Yo, who is calling that weasel?"

"I don't know, but let's go stand over on the west side and find out." They weren't being nosy, just trying to stay on point. Information could get twisted up faster than gossip at a woman's hair salon in the pen. Men were lip runners too. Sometimes worse than the chattiest females. Nasty didn't want information unless it was firsthand. He'd rather hear for himself than through inmate.com.

Shorty 55 was seated on the edge of his unmade bunk with a wicky over the window. He'd just did a li'l dope and had his dick out and was stroking himself into ecstasy when he heard his name being called. He was just a few moments away from the climax when someone knocked on his door. They fucked up his high.

"I'm taking a shit. What?" he said, holding back his moans of pleasure as he stroked himself. He sped up the momentum because he didn't want to miss a good one. "Uggh, ahh!" he said lowly as his bodily fluids jolted into his hands. He flushed the toilet, and then wiped his hands on the sides of shorts, leaving sticky residue everywhere. Finally, he opened the door.

"Yo, 55, somebody want you at the window."

55 stepped out of his cell and let the man lead him to the window. He was soon met by his protection. Four huge-ass dudes that should have been playing for the Baltimore Ravens' defense line instead of doing life in prison.

"Who is it?" 55 asked his man. Apple, the man who delivered the message and 55's top security guy, shrugged his big-ass shoulders.

Shorty 55 made his way to the window. High on heroin, he struggled to make out the figure 75 feet away from him, outside, standing behind a barbed wire fence. He squeezed his ugly face between the bars as best he could and squinted his eyes to get a better look. But it was useless. The black-clad figure was too hard to make out.

"Yeah, this 55. What's happening?" he asked screaming down to the sidewalk.

"Have you spoken to your sons?"

"My sons? What you asking 'bout my sons for? Who you?"

"Listen, 55—and listen to me real good . . . You fucked up."

"*I* fucked up?" 55 said smiling, revealing two missing front teeth. The rest of his grill looked like the color of a rotting banana.

"Yes, you did. You see, you took a chain from a very good friend of mine. And you need to give it back. You got 24 hours to return it. You can simply give it to his son. Because if you don't, each one of your sons will die, one by one."

Shorty 55 snapped his head back.

"Hold the fuck up! You threatening me, clown? Muthafucka, you putting a death threat on my sons over a chain?" Shorty 55 smiled. "Y'all trying to play me like a bitch! You got the wrong nigga. I run *this* pen."

"You might run the pen, but *we* run these streets!" Moon said.

"What if I told you I already sold that chain? I ripped the little ugly-ass picture off and sold that gold."

By now, the whole west wing was listening to their open-air dispute. Even people on the street were listening. But Moon was through talking. He turned his head toward the van that was parked behind him and signaled for it to pull up.

"Bring 'im out!" Moon said. His man opened the van door. He dragged a man out and stood him up straight. It was John, Shorty 55's little brother. "Say hello to your brother!"

"My brother? John! John, that's you?" 55 asked. But there was no response other than the sound of the MAC-10. John's head exploded into shreds as the clip was emptied into his dome and chest, bloodying up the sidewalk.

"Twenty-four hours, bitch!" And they jumped in the trucks and sped off.

Nasty heard the shots . . . the whole conversation, for that matter. He smiled to himself knowing that his man Soulja had not let him down. Nasty had nothing to do with orchestrating this. It was Soulja. And just that fast, their reign had been solidified, killing off any lingering doubt because there was no retaliation. It was done in such a way that it could not legally be brought back to Nasty or any of his men. This was street shit. By the time the police came running to lock down the prison, Nasty and Rocky had exchanged nods. They were not to be fucked with by any means. Shorty 55 knew that whoever did this meant business. He could assume it was Nasty and/or Soulja, but Mo Garrett had so much love in the pen and in the streets, it really could have been anybody.

Nasty closed his eyes and spoke to Mo Garrett. "I know none of this can bring you back. But I know if you're watching, you can damn surely say we tried to level the scales."

CHAPTER 21

The music was making the whole place vibrate. The Pretty Avenue, a poppin' strip club in Baltimore, was packed. Mad-Dog and Paige were sitting in VIP, all over each other. They were falling in love and didn't care who knew it. Mad-Dog had damn near bought out the bar, showing out for his lady.

At the same time, Tony felt that it was time for him to show Paige what he was working with. He saw on Instagram that they were at The Pretty Avenue. So he hopped in his Range and made his way there. He wanted to be seen. He wanted her to feel his presence. Tony walked in and immediately spotted change. They briefly locked eyes. He nodded his head respectfully and dipped in the opposite direction. She noticed him shining. Tony had on a few diamond-clad chains, a stunning pinky ring, with a matching bracelet, a shining Rolex, and a $3,000 pair of Louis Vuitton sneakers.

His plan was to walk over to them and give Paige $10,000 for her and Tonaya. But he was having a hard time getting past the way she allowed Mad-Dog to touch her. He was claiming her hard. And it was killing Tony. But he already knew what he was walking into when he entered the spot. He swallowed his pride and turned to head in their direction.

"Your boy is on his way over here, baby girl. I hope he comes on his best behavior," Mad-Dog said to Paige. Her breath was caught in her throat. Tony did not look like himself. He had a different energy. A different swag. He was more confident. He was being escorted by one of the bouncers. This time he didn't have to get permission to enter VIP. He had his own section across from Mad-Dog and Paige.

He stepped into the VIP area. "Paige, I need to talk to you."

"Tony, there ain't nothing for us to talk about."

"What you mean there's nothing for us to talk about? We have a daughter. Tonaya is plenty to talk about," he said. Paige rolled her eyes and turned to face Mad-Dog and laughed at a joke that nobody heard but her. Mad-Dog whispered in her ear.

"Baby, don't be childish. Go talk to the man. It's all good. I'll be right here." She looked at him and nodded. Then she got up and went to talk to Tony.

"First and foremost, I want to give you this," he handed her the money. He did in such a way that he knew Mad-Dog saw him. She looked at the money. "Put that away," he said. She stuck it in her purse.

"Tony, this shit don't make up for what you did."

"I know. But I need to make sure you and Tonaya are good. I'ma have some more to give you in a little bit."

"All right. Bye, Tony."

"Hold up," he said. "We still got more to talk about. I . . ." Tony really didn't know what else to say. Paige folder her arms. Before Tony could say anything else, he was tapped on his shoulder by someone.

"Whattup, Tone!" It was none other than Rodney and his brother Bishop.

"Man, don't whattup me, nigga. Me and you got some issues to discuss."

"Issues? Fuck you talkin' 'bout, li'l nigga?"

"Li'l nigga? What type of shit you on, Rodney? I thought me and you had a deal. You told me that Baltimore Ave. was mine. Yet, you pushed my men off and been getting money over there. I brang that clientele. We could have eaten together; all we had to do was discuss. I don't know if I like the way you do business, Rod."

Paige couldn't believe the conversation happening in front of her. This was not the Tony she knew, although she was proud of him for standing up for himself—even if he was a cheater.

"First of all, Rodney, if you had any respect, you would wait and have this conversation later. Don't you see us talking?" Paige couldn't stand Rodney for what he did to Von. And pieces of hate spit out of her mouth and smacked him with every word she spoke.

"Listen, nobody is talking to you; mind your own business, Paige," Rodney said. Now Mad-Dog stood up ready to pounce on Rodney.

"Fuck you, Rod. You ain't nothing but a bitch-ass nigg—" before Paige could get the words out of her mouth, Bishop, Rodney's brother, swung on Tony.

She wasn't sure if it was a reflex action or what, but she didn't even have time to think about it. The bottle of Ace of Spades sitting on the table next to where they were standing was now in her hand, swinging through the air until it collided with Bishop's head. It knocked him to the ground. And now Rodney was up in Paige's face, pushing up on her as though he might touch her. But that only lasted for half a second because Tony and Mad-Dog were both all on him like he was a gazelle and they were fierce lions. All of Mad-Dogs men got involved trying to neutralize the situation. But an all-out war was going on inside the club.

Bishop wasn't done. He was a little stunned from the bottle hitting him in the head, but he was otherwise okay. While on the ground, he touched the top of his head, and felt blood. He ignored all the other craziness going on around him and honed in on Paige—going straight for her.

Mad-Dog and Tony, with their men, were so busy getting at Rodney, that the short time that they took their eyes off Paige proved detrimental. Bishop discreetly got up and ran toward her, punching Paige in the face so hard, it knocked her unconscious. Something in Tony jumped and caused him to turn around. He saw Paige lying on the floor, people stepping over her to get out of the club. His heart jumped in his chest. This wasn't even his beef, but Paige was *his* girl now. He saw Bishop's slimy ass trying to sneak out of the club. Mad-Dog had a pocketknife, and he pulled it out while running in the direction of Bishop.

When Mad-Dog caught up with Bishop, he transformed into the devil. He dug deep into Bishop's ribs with the small yet deadly dagger. Then he pulled it out and jabbed him in his back. It wasn't long before Rodney's men peeped what was happening and swarmed Mad-Dog. Mad-Dog was handling business, reminding everybody why he had that name in the first place.

The bouncers were catching hell trying to end the brawl. Blood was everywhere. It seemed like it wouldn't end, and then it did—when six shots were fired. Then there was more screaming and more running. Tony dragged Paige's limp body behind the bar and tried to wake her up. She stirred, but she was dazed. There was blood trailing behind her head. He figured that when she hit the floor, she must have cracked the back of her head.

He threw her over his shoulder and intended to put her in his car. But as soon as he stepped outside the back door, Mad-Dog was there. "I'll take it from here," he said. Tony wanted to protest, but Mad-Dog stood his ground. He passed a barely conscious Paige to him.

"You going to the hospital, right, fam?" Tony asked, concerned. Mad-Dog walked fast to his truck carrying Paige. He ignored Tony. Just 'cause they brawled together didn't mean they were friends. "Yo!" Tony called out again. "I'm not trying to beef with you, Mad-Dog, but that's the mother of my daughter. I need to know she's gonna be all right."

"Of course I'm taking her to the hospital," he said without turning around. He threw Paige in the backseat and sped off. Tony could barely breathe.

The hospital's emergency room was packed that night. It must've been a full moon. When Von called Marla and told her to meet her at the hospital due to an emergency, Marla panicked. She was hoping that Von hadn't taken a turn for the worst because the urgency in Von's voice shook Marla to the core. The baby? The illness? Marla didn't know what to expect.

Marla came running into the emergency room. But she stopped dead in her tracks when she saw Mad-Dog and Von standing next to each other. Mad-Dog had blood on his shirt.

"What the fuck happened?" Marla asked.

"I can't be here right now. They got cameras in here and shit. I just need to make sure Paige is good. Y'all stay here with her. I'll call you in a minute, Von," Mad-Dog said, and then he walked out of the ER. The bulge in his back let all know he was carrying.

"Von, what the fuck?" Marla asked, confused.

"Mad-Dog said that him and Paige were out at the club. Then Tony showed up and him and Paige were speaking about something."

"Oh God, did Mad-Dog do something to Tony?"

"No, Rodney showed up in there, and him and Tony got into it."

"Rodney and Tony? What they got beef for?"

"Something about territory. I don't know. But Rodney's brother Bishop attacked Tony, and Paige hit him over the head with a bottle. Then he got up and knocked Paige out. She hit her head on the floor and might have a concussion. Plus, she was drinking, so you know that made it worse."

"I can't believe this shit. If it ain't one thing, it's another!" Von said. Just then, the doctor came out. He walked over to Von, and then Marla grabbed her hand, hoping for the best.

"Your friend is going to be just fine," the doctor said. "We'll keep her a day for observation, and then she can go home and she'll be just fine."

"Thank God!" Von said out loud. If it isn't one thing,

it's another. That seemed to be their motto.

CHAPTER 22

Soulja called Nasty's cell phone. "I was waiting to hear from you, brother," Nasty said.

"I'm sure," Soulja responded.

"So check this out, the chain was in my locker when I came back from the yard," Nasty informed.

"That's what was supposed to happen. I'm happy to hear it."

"Yo, brother that was honor how you handled the situation," Nasty said.

"No question. But I'm telling you right now, that's it. Everything needs to be peace."

"I think it will be from here on out."

"What you mean you think?" Soulja asked.

"Well, right before you called, I found out that Shorty 55 wants to talk to me on the yard. What you think?"

"What's the setup?"

"The Muslim brothers are all out there. They got the yard secured. He called them there to let me know it wasn't no tricky shit going on."

"A'ight. Well, go. And make sure you let him know he don't run shit no more."

"Oh, most definitely. I'ma make sure that he crawls up in his shell this time."

At that moment, Soulja heard the guards calling his name. "Listen, you be safe. I'll hit you back later. I got a visit. I don't know who the hell came out here to Louisiana to see me, but I'm grateful, even if it is a surprise."

"That's love. Okay, brother, I'll kick it with you later."

Soulja quickly showered and went down to the visiting room. He was happy that he went to the barber yesterday, got a fresh shape up and his hair recornrowed. Soulja had long straight-back cornrows that reached to the middle of his back. He kept it neat because his hair was very soft, and he didn't like the rough, frizzy look. He was a very neat and clean man. But, if necessary, he *could* get dirty.

He optimistically walked into the visiting room, wondering who made the long trip. He looked around and spotted a familiar face. It was his little sister. Not by blood, but a sister, nonetheless. Von. Von had come to see him. *Wow*, was all he thought. He hadn't seen her in a long time. And he was smiling from ear to ear. He looked around to see if Marla was with her, maybe in the bathroom or at the vending machine, but he quickly realized by the way their chairs were arranged that Von had made the trip alone.

"What you doing here, girl?" he said hugging her, then kissing her forehead. She hugged him back tightly. He noticed how big she was.

"I just needed to get away from all the craziness. I hopped on a plane, and here I am."

"Well, I feel honored," Soulja admitted.

"And look at your hair. It's so long," she said.

"Something to do to kill the time."

"Well, you look very handsome, bro. I miss you," she said.

"I miss you too with your big self. If I didn't know any better, I would think you're pregnant," he said, fishing. There was a brief silence between them. Then Von held her head down.

"I am."

"I am *what?*" he said, not wanting to believe what his eyes and ears were now confirming.

"Pregnant."

"Von . . . damn, Von. Does Nasty know? Well, wait. I know he doesn't because he would have told me."

"Nah, he doesn't know and can't know."

"It is what it is now. There's no reason for it to be a secret. How far are you?" He put his hand on her stomach.

"I'm 5 months," she said looking at her feet.

"Von, you're grown. So I'm not gonna lecture you. Hold your head up. But for the record, don't keep nothing else from me. When you fought with Rodney that time and wrote me about it, I never told Nasty. I knew that crazy nicca couldn't handle it. I just gave you advice."

"Don't try to play all innocent, I knew it wasn't a coincidence that somebody rear-ended him a week after I told you, and then dragged him out of the car and stomped him out."

"Nah, that wasn't me," Soulja said with a slick smile on his face. Von punched his arm playfully. "So, you're really having a baby, huh? You ready to do this? I know you and Rod aren't together."

For some reason, Von felt like she was just 9 years old in his presence. She looked up at him. He noticed there were tears in her eyes. He wiped them.

"Don't cry, li'l sis. It's gonna all work out. Nasty will be out soon if his wild ass chills out. You won't be alone. He'll be happy to help you and raise his niece or nephew with you."

"I know," she said wiping her eyes.

"It's okay. I promise you it will work out."

"I just never expected to be an unmarried, single mother."

"Shit happens, Von. You know, most of the time the

good girls get the short end of the stick. I don't understand it myself, but I put Keva through a lot of shit. I treated her like she was a piece of meat. And now look, she's raising my daughter and ended up being extremely valuable in my life. The jewel is, you never know who you might need. Treat everybody with respect unless they disrespect you."

"Why do men do this type of this shit?" Von said, confused. "Especially when they have a woman who loves them and stays loyal."

"It's the streets. The streets do it to us. It's not until situations like this that a man learns the true value of a woman—when one is completely deprived of her essence."

"It's almost like a good black man is impossible to find."

"Not impossible, but close to it. Many good men are locked down. But you gotta remember our history, baby girl. I read a lot about our people. Our men were forced to be breeders back in slave days. We had to disconnect from women, because our wives, our children could be sold at any given moment. So we taught ourselves not to care. Not to love. It was a survival mechanism, and the boys learned it from the men, until it became cultural. Be a breeder, not a lover. It fucked us up. And after 400 years of that, this is what you get. A bunch of confused men."

"Wow. You're so smart, bro. I love the way you always break things down to me." She touched her belly and looked down at it. "Uncle Soulja is gonna teach you a bunch of stuff," she said to her baby. Then she looked back up at him. "The way you explained it, I guess I never looked at it that way before. But that makes sense. Maybe one day I'll forgive him."

"When you have your baby, if it's a boy, teach him how to love a woman the right way, so he doesn't make the mistakes his father is making." This made Von love Soulja even more. She wished there were men like him out there.

"Well, let me tell you what's been going on. There was big-ass fight that jumped off the other day at The Pretty Avenue. Tony was fighting Rodney's crew, and so was Mad-Dog. Then they went crazy because this chick got knocked out. It was a trip."

Immediately Soulja looked perplexed. "What chick?"

"Well, I didn't wanna say nothing, but I'd rather tell you before my brother finds out. It was Paige!"

"Paige?! Fuck is you talkin' 'bout, Von? Paige? A nicca put their hands on Paige?" Anger rushed over Soulja like a tsunami. Von put her hand on his shoulder and explained the whole story.

"It was crazy," she said when she was done.

"So, basically, she got hit because she came to Tony's defense? I thought Paige was through with him. And what was Tony doing up in The Pretty Avenue anyway? That ain't never been his type of crowd."

"Tony is getting big dope money now. He blew up. He's

even pushing a brand-new Range Rover, and he copped Sharise a 650 BMW."

"I didn't know he was getting down like that."

"Yeah, it almost happened overnight."

"So did Paige fall for the game? Did she get all open off his new look?"

"Nah. She is still rocking with Mad-Dog."

"Good. I told her if she was gonna move on with a man like that to keep it one hundred. Yo is a real G. He move like a young Soulja, so I respect his handle. Men like that are not to be played with. Not their money, their family, or their feelings. But enough about that, what up with you? Are you doing okay? You seem real down, baby girl."

"I gotta tell you some things, Soulja. I needed to talk to someone I could trust."

"You already know that you got that with me. You're just as much of a sister to me as you are to Nasty. So spill it, girl."

"Okay. Damn, I don't even know how to say this."

"Is it something that Nasty already knows?" Soulja asked.

"Hell, no! And he can never know. You gotta promise me on your life that you won't tell Nasty. And you gotta promise it will stay between us, no matter what. Take it to your grave. And you can't harm nobody."

"Well, I can promise you not to tell nobody, but I can't

promise you I won't harm nobody. You're scaring me, Von. What the hell is up? "

"I just don't want you worrying about me."

"That's automatic. Now spill it and stop playing with me."

She closed her eyes and exhaled. "Soulja, Rodney gave me HIV, and the medicine doesn't work for me," she said. She'd been lying to her friends. Von was dying.

"No, Von. No!" Soulja said getting up from his seat and biting his fist. He wanted to explode from the inside out. Not his baby. Not li'l Von. He'd seen hundreds of fiends come in the prison, sick from the disease. He'd seen the worst side of it. Not Von. This couldn't be. He sat back down. Von began to cry.

"I'm sorry, bro. I'm so sorry. I should have stopped messing with him once I found out he was cheating so bad. I shouldn't have stayed. But I loved him. I loved him so much. He was all I had out here. All I had."

Soulja couldn't believe what Von had just laid on him. She was carrying a baby. And neither of them might live since the medicine didn't work. This was the epitome of foulness.

"There is nothing for you to be sorry about. Come here," he said grabbing her and hugging her. He let her sob on his chest. He whispered in her ear, "That bitch gotta die! I'ma kill him my muh-fucking self if these pigs grants my appeal. But he's a dead nigga, either way."

AISHA HALL WITH WEEDIE

CHAPTER 23

After the fight at the strip club, Tony got home and began suffering from severe headaches. During the brawl at the club, he hit his head. When the pain became unbearable, he went to the hospital. They did an MRI and wanted to keep him for observation.

He called Paige to check on her and make sure she was okay. She was home now. But now he was in the hospital, and he wanted her to bring their daughter Tonaya to see him. He hadn't seen her in a long time, and it was beginning to wear on him. Paige agreed, and he waited patiently. Paige didn't want to go, but Marla convinced her and even came with her. She promised to wait in the waiting room.

About an hour later, the door to his room flew open, and Tonaya came sprinting to him. "Daddy!" He got up and picked up his baby girl, kissing her forehead and spinning her around. He sat down quickly because his head was ringing.

"Did you miss Daddy?" he asked, still planting kisses.

"Yes, I missed you so much. Mommy said you ran away from us and you were being a bad daddy. Are you gonna come back?" she asked. Paige stood at the door with her hand on her hip watching them.

"So that's what you was telling my baby? That I ran away from her? That's foul, Paige."

"Just enjoy your baby," she said. Paige looked at the two of them interacting and missed her family. But she wasn't about to forgive Tony for what he did—abandoning her and Tonaya for a known hooker and thief. When Paige finally walked into the room, Tony could still see that her face was a little swollen from being hit so hard by Bishop. It made his headache come on that much stronger. He hated the idea of someone hurting her.

"Daddy, you hurt?"

"No, I'm okay."

"You seen the doctor yet?"

"Yup. I'll be leaving later." Tonaya examined her father herself, checking his legs and arms for any further damage. While she probed, Tony figured he would too. "So you all right, Paige?" he asked.

"How do I look?" she said right back, then rolling her eyes.

"Well, you look better than I do, I'm sure. And thank you for coming to my aid. You were the last person I expected to help me."

Paige walked over to him and put Tonaya into the chair beside the bed. Tony reached up and grabbed Paige, hugging her. She hugged him back, and then put her arms down, but Tony wouldn't let go. He was on the verge of tears. He realized how much he loved Paige, and his love seemed to have grown even deeper since the last time he touched her.

"Let go," she whispered, not wanting Tonaya to hear, who was now playing one of the games on Paige's phone.

"Paige, I'm not letting go. Just say the word. Just say it, baby, and it's done. Sharise. The game. Everything. I love you. Love my family," he said. She backed away from him and sat on the edge of the bed. He sat beside her.

"Just let us go, Tony. I thought about it, but the trust is gone. I do not trust you, and I never will."

"A man is supposed to be allowed to correct his mistakes, right, Paige?"

"A man is also supposed to be able to accept the repercussions that comes with the life he chooses to live. You cheated on me, Tony. For no reason. I'm not enough for you, obviously."

"That's not true." He stroked her hair, and Tonaya watched. She didn't understand what they were talking about, but she could feel the love in the room. She got up and sat between them.

"It's true."

"I'm sorry, Paige. I'm sorry, baby." He rubbed her lips with his finger. He used to do it all the time. Paige loved Tony. She could feel how sorry he was, and she was trying hard to be hard. She knew he was hurting; she'd never seen him so vulnerable. His eyes were glassy. She could tell he was fighting with all his strength to hold back the tears. Then she looked beside the bed on the table and saw the keys to his Range Rover and another set of keys that had a BMW logo. Her anger flared. She got up from the bed.

Just then, Sharise walked into the room, saying, "Baby, how are you feeling?" She walked over to Tony, kissing him on the mouth. Tony pushed her back slightly and looked over at Tonaya who had a disgusted yet confused look on her young face.

"Daddy, who is that?" she asked.

"I'm Sharise," she said.

"Don't you dare speak to my daughter."

Sharise just smiled. She and Paige locked eyes. "Am I interrupting something here?" she asked.

"You're not interrupting anything. We were just leaving," Paige said. "Come on Tonaya."

"Hold up!" Tony said in protest. "I haven't seen Tonaya in months, and you're ready to take her already."

"That's all the time you needed, obviously. Go ahead and chill with Sharise."

"Leave my name outta your mouth, ma. You're not in

my league, boo." Sharise said. Just then Marla walked into the room. She'd seen Sharise come in and wanted to make sure her girl was good.

"You're right, Sharise, I'm *not* in your league. I'm a *lady*, and I don't weigh my worth on material things."

"Bitch, *please*. You're just jealous because your baby father paid almost 50 stacks for this 650 I've got, and you ain't get $650 to spend."

"Would y'all stop the stupid shit!"

Paige was almost knocked off her feet by the power of Tony's words.

"Stupid shit? Why don't you just be quiet, Tony? It's *your* fault that this bitch is feeling herself in the first place."

"Who are you calling a bitch, Paige? You better check your tongue since your lips is already swollen," Sharise smirked.

"That's 'cause I loved that nicca enough to go to war with him. Where the fuck was you when shit popped off? Somewhere being the bum that you are?"

"Nah, actually, I was at home waiting in the bed for him to come back so I could ride that good dick." Tonaya covered her ears.

"That's what sluts do."

"Keep talking, Paige, and I'ma show you what sluts *really* do. I will *rip* your face off, bitch."

Tonaya started crying. That's when Marla picked her up

and took her out of the room. Then she came right back in with her earrings off.

"Your threats don't mean nothing to me. Do you know who my brothers are? Bitch, fuck you and Tony. I could make a phone call and have both y'all heads hit." She then turned to Tony. "But you know what? I love Tony. So, Tony, go ahead and tell her that you want your family back, and then you can have me and Tonaya back just like you want." Tony looked at Tonaya in the corner looking scared and confused, then at Paige's beautiful face.

"I love you, Paige. And I'll do anything to have my family back!"

"What? Oh no, your ass didn't just cross me, Tony! You're a bona fide sucker-ass nigga. Fuck you!"

Paige smiled and walked over to Tony. She kissed him hard on the mouth. Tony held onto her, but then Paige pushed him away.

"Fuck both y'all fleas. Y'all belong together. I just wanted to show you where you stand with him, Sharise. A filler. Just something to do. You called me bitch, but you said it wrong. I'm a *bad* bitch and don't you *ever* forget it, boo boo."

"Paige!" Tony said. He couldn't believe she played him like that.

"Payback is a bitch, ain't doe?" She walked over to Tonaya and stuck her hand out. "Come on, baby. Let's go. Daddy is busy right now." Tonaya sadly waved good-bye to her father. Marla joined them, and the crew of three left the hospital room.

"That was some cold shit, Paige. But I *liked* it," Marla said in disbelief.

"You wanna play with fire, sometimes you get burnt!" Paige said.

"Very true."

Paige opened the back door to Mad-Dog's arctic-white 600 Benz and strapped Tonaya in. She felt good as a muh'fucker!

CHAPTER 24

Three months passed since the crazy fight at The Pretty Avenue. Von's phone rang one day. It was Nasty. She was happy he called before she got to the doctor's office. She didn't want to talk to him while she was there.

"Happy birthday, little sister."

"Thank you, twin. I'm almost 20."

"I know, don't remind me. What y'all doing? I know you got something planned."

"Actually, I'm hanging out with Paige and Mad-Dog tonight. Mad-Dog is doing something. I thought that was nice of him."

"Yeah, Paige got herself a good man."

"So how is everything going in there?"

"Everything is good. The beef is straight. Shorty 55 seen that the beef got taken to the street, so he fell back. All is peace here. Hopefully, no more blood will shed."

"Good, because I can't wait for you to get out here." Von was happy to know that Soulja had obviously kept her secret. She was expected to go into labor in just a few weeks. They ended the call. Von continued to get ready for whatever surprise Mad-Dog had for her. He was a very nice dude, and Von was extremely happy for her friend.

As she was applying lip gloss, she got a phone call. She thought it was Nasty calling back, but then she realized it wasn't 15 minutes yet. The number said **unavailable**.

"Hello!"

"Von! Whattup?" It was Rodney. She frowned up her face.

"What?" she said.

"How are you? I saw you yesterday coming from church. Wow, you are so big."

"Most pregnant women are."

"Listen, Von, when is the next time you go to the doctor about the baby?" He was clear to say "about the baby," not wanting to mislead Von into thinking he accepted that he had the disease.

"Actually, I go today."

"I wanna go with you. Can I pick you up?" Von didn't want to be anywhere with him, but he *was* the father of her child, and he'd been asking her for months to go with her.

"Fine, Rodney. But you gotta be here in 20 minutes." She hung up, and Rod was outside in no more than 5 minutes. She was happy that Paige and Marla weren't home at the time. She didn't want to hear their mouths about her going anywhere with him.

"Hi, Von!" Dr. Maru said. "And who is this?"

"This is Rodney. The father of my baby."

"Oh! Rodney. Pleased to meet you." She put her hand out to shake his, and he just looked at her. Von cleared her throat. "Alrighty, well, did you come in to get tested today?" the doctor asked.

"Tested? Nah, I'm good."

"No, you're not good, young man. Von has HIV, and if you're admittedly the father of this baby, then you need to be tested."

Rod didn't feel like arguing with the lady, so he rolled up his sleeve and let her draw a small amount of blood. She left the room, and when she returned, she told Von to get undressed and then sit on the examination table.

"How long is this gonna take?" he asked. His mood was ruined now that this woman had taken his blood.

"Not long," Von said looking at Rodney, him wondering how she ever loved this monster.

Von got on the table, and the doctor rubbed clear gel on her large stomach. "Okay, we're going to now hear the baby's heartbeat." Swoosh, wush. *Swoosh, wush, wush, wush.* The doctor had a perplexed look on her face.

"What's wrong?" Von said, feeling that the doctor had noticed something wrong.

Dr. Maru then moved the ultrasound around to the bottom of Von's stomach. "Arch your back slightly for a moment," the doctor said. She looked at the screen again, and then put her hand over her mouth.

"Please tell me what's wrong," Von begged.

"Yeah, what's up, Doc?" Rod said, curiously.

"Is there something wrong with my baby?" Von asked nervously. "I can handle it. Just please tell me," she said desperately.

"Well, it's not your baby. It's *babies*. You have two fetuses, Von. One is much smaller than the other, and it looks like one's been hiding behind the other. That's why we couldn't see it before. And their heartbeats were probably in sync before, so we didn't pick up on it. But, yes, there are two babies here. My God!"

"Two?" Von said. "Are you playing a joke on me?"

"I'm about to have *two* babies! *That's* what I'm talking about!" Rodney shouted. He felt that only a real man could make *two* babies at the same time. So he injected himself with a shot of superego. Dr. Maru was not smiling.

"I'm sorry to tell you, but one baby has been getting most of the nutrients. The other has not developed at the same rate. It's probably due to complications from your illness. We will do all we can to save both babies."

Von wiped her eyes. She didn't know how much more of this she could take. It was like a cruel joke.

"What a birthday gift. Two children," Rod said with his ignorant ass. Von was in disbelief. The horror story could not have gotten any worse. All she needed now was to go into labor on Friday the thirteenth, and then maybe she would see the humor in the whole dark thing.

After speaking with the doctor about the babies, Von found out she was having a girl and the other sex was unknown. The doctor could not get a clear view of the other one. Von didn't care. She just wanted to do all that she could to bring them into this world as healthy as possible.

"Mr. Rodney, can you please come to the back office so I can discuss the results of your test."

"Nah. Hold dat! Come on, Von. Let's go."

"I strongly suggest you come to the back." The doctor wanted to yell out to him that he was positive, but she couldn't violate HIPAA laws and expose his personal medical records. She could lose her license, and this asshole wasn't worth that. And she couldn't report him, because if he wasn't aware of the disease due to being told the results, technically, he wasn't responsible. At least not legally.

"It's all right, Dr. Maru. Thank you. I'll be back next week like you said."

She kissed Von on the cheek. Von was such a sweet girl, and Dr. Maru hated that she'd been involved with a man like Rodney. All she could do was shake her head when they left.

Von didn't let the news ruin her birthday. Instead, she embraced it and believed that this must be God's will. She waited at home with her girls for Mad-Dog to pick them up. He rolled up with a bunch of people. An entourage followed them on the highway as Mad-Dog led the way to Hanover, Pennsylvania.

"Where are we going, baby?" Paige asked.

"You'll see. It's a surprise!"

For a moment, Von envied Paige. She had a man who loved her and treated her like a queen. She knew that would never happen for her.

Finally, they arrived. They pulled up in front of a big mansion. There were a few cars already parked in different directions in the roundabout driveway.

"This, this is my house!"

"What?" Paige said. "No-fucking-way!"

"I got a good deal on it a while back, and I've been sitting on it. I had no reason to come out here, but now I do." They all stepped out of the vehicles. "I hope you'll move here with me, Paige." Paige was shocked. Her girls started clapping and talking shit.

"Bitch, you better pack your shit. I'll help you. This right here is a castle," her friend Keisha said.

"For real, girl. I wish I had a place like this to call home," Nicole added. These were Paige and Von's friends that came along for the ride to celebrate Von's birthday.

"I don't know what to say," Paige said. "This is—"

"Don't say nothing right now. Just think about it. But there's a real nice room that Tonaya would love. Come inside so I can show it to you," he said winking at her.

"They know good and well they going in there to do the nasty," Sconey added, whispering to Von. Paige grabbed hold of Mad-Dog's hand, and he led the way into the huge house. Paige thought to herself that Maddie seemed too good to be true. Move in with him? But really, Paige already knew her answer was no. She would never leave Von. Her home was with Von and Marla. There was no changing that. But she was flattered by what Mad-Dog had done.

The party was fun. There were about 15 of them celebrating Von's life. Just 19, and so beautiful. Huge, but beautiful. There was a cake that Mad-Dog had gotten made which was a miniature version of Von. Pregnant belly and all. It was so cute. It must've cost a fortune.

"Okay, it's gift exchange time," Marla said. "I wanna give my gift first."

"No, I want to give her mines first," Paige said, shoving Marla out of the way.

WAHIDA CLARK PRESENTS : BALTIMORE RAW

"Hold on, I have something to tell everyone first before we start gift exchanging. I have the biggest gift of them all."

"It's your birthday. You're not supposed to be giving out gifts," Marla said.

"Well, this gift is for everyone. Okay, well, I found out something amazing today."

"What?" Paige asked with her eyebrows raised.

"There is going to be another baby added to the family." Everybody looked at Paige.

"Don't look at me. I am not pregnant."

"Not yet," Mad-Dog said, standing behind her kissing her neck.

"Seriously, it's not me. Marla, you pregnant? You been getting it in in the visits with Nasty? Let me find out."

"You'll are a trip. No! It's me!"

"We already know you're having a baby. What you talking about, girl?"

"I'm pregnant with twins!"

"Twins? Stop playing with us, Von!" Paige said.

"Nah, I mean it. The way they were positioned made it hard to see the other one. And their heartbeats were in sync, so the doctor couldn't hear two heartbeats. But I heard it today. There's two of them. I'm having two babies."

Everybody clapped and congratulated her except for Marla and Paige. They were the only two that understood the seriousness of this situation. Von simply exhaled and said, "Well, better than any gift you have here tonight, Marla and Paige, if you would be the godmothers, nothing would make me happier."

"Of course, we will," they both said. They hugged their friend and tried to appear to be to be happy, but they were both sad as hell.

CHAPTER 25

Sharise had not seen Tony in days. She was hurt and humiliated that he chose that bitch Paige over her. But Sharise was the payback queen. So rather than cry about it, she'd just get even. First, she met up with Bishop. She got his number from a friend and told him that she wanted to talk to him about a business proposition. He was weaker than Rodney, and she figured her way in was through him. Turns out she was right. Bishop and Rodney were brothers, and she knew that she could turn them against Tony even more. Besides, Bishop was cuter than Rodney in Sharise's opinion, and she knew he would be ready to get some payback when it came to Tony since the beef was originally between him and Rodney. She played her cards just right and landed herself in Bishop's bed. Then his head, making him think he was the king of the world.

"Bishop, you're sticking this dick to me, baby. Oh my God! I'm coming again! Again!"

"Me too, baby. Me too. I'm 'bout to bust all up in that pussy, baby," Bishop whispered.

Sharise lifted herself up off of his dick and grabbed his nature real tight at the base.

"Sharise why did you stop? I was about to come, baby."

"I need this shit to stay hard, Bishop. I'm still horny and want more," Sharise said going up and down on him with her mouth and making loud noises when she pulled up off of it. She went back down like the drop from a roller coaster, deep throating him and caressing his nuts all at the same time.

"Damn, ma! You are the best. Word! I wish you were my girl. We were made for each other."

"Climb on top of my face, Bish, and put it in my mouth." Bishop obeyed. "Oh yeah, baby, that's right. I love the feeling of you stretching my throat," she said between strokes. Sharise was a top-notch freak. And that's how she sucked Tony in. Her sex skills had gotten her through most of her life.

"Damn, Sharise! Fuck!" he said reacting to her perfected suction. They locked eyes, and Sharise stopped his stroke to run her tongue across his shaft.

"You can have it any way you want it, baby."

Suddenly there was a sound in the house that startled them. Then the bedroom door flew open. It was Rodney.

"What the hell is going on up in here?" he said. Sharise had wrapped herself in a sheet at this point. "What's going on?" he asked again.

"What it look like?" Sharise said sarcastically. When Rod saw the outline of her body through the sheet, his manhood instantly got hard. He wanted some of what his brother had.

"Bro, you feeling stingy, or you wanna share?" Rod asked.

"What makes you think it's up to him?" Sharise stated matter-of-factly.

"It's not! It depends if you wanna get freaked for real, baby." Rodney began rubbing his crotch. Bishop laid her back and began encircling her vagina with his tongue. Sharise could not contain herself. She began moaning and making sucking sounds with her mouth. Rodney was beside himself. He came over to her and began sucking on her nipple. Sharise had never had two men at the same time. Being the freak she was, she welcomed it, having no idea she was playing with fire. In the next minute, Rodney was naked right along with his brother.

"Let me finish what I started," she said to Bishop. Bishop had a big dick, and she assumed they both would since they were brothers. She began sucking Bishop again, and while Bishop got pleased, so did Sharise. Rodney took over where his brother left off and began licking Sharise's clit, and then eventually put his tongue deep inside her. Her moans were relentless. And without warning, right when she was about to climax, Rodney rammed his dick inside of her. It felt so good, she didn't stop him and make him put on a condom. She took his sick dick and grinded on it, while his brother released his juices inside her mouth.

The three of them sat in the kitchen, all of them smoking cigarettes. Sharise was still naked, doing everything in her power to get Rodney and Bishop to play along with her antics. "So what brings you over here? You trying to make peace so we don't kill your nigga for starting all that shit at The Pretty Avenue?"

"I'm not with Tony anymore. He's a bitch. A wannabe. He can't even handle the shit on his couple of blocks."

"He looks to be handling just fine to me," he said. Rodney wasn't buying it. He got up from the table calmly and walked behind Sharise who was still sitting and smoking. Then he grabbed her by her throat and put her in a headlock.

"Bitch, you trying to set me up? What the fuck you really want over here? Where's Tony. He 'bout to try to run up in here while you got us off our square? That's the oldest trick in the book, baby, and it ain't happening over here," Rod said.

"No! No!" Sharise said. She could barely talk, Rodney was squeezing her neck so tight.

"Say that again?" he said.

"I said . . . no!" He released his grip some.

"How I know you not on some bullshit."

"I'm not. I'm not with Tony anymore. I can prove it." This got his attention. He released her. But this time he took out a gun from the kitchen cabinet. Bishop stayed quiet.

"I am not with him. I was, but he said he wanted his baby mama back. That bitch Paige. We were all at the hospital, and he shitted on me right in front her. So fuck him."

"Still, how do I know your ass ain't lying?"

"Because, I know where his stash is, and I want you to rob him."

"Why don't you do it yourself?" he asked.

"I can't. He would know. I want you to put a gun to my head, take me to his house, and make it look like you forced me. He has surveillance, and he'll see you holding me at gunpoint. He won't come for you. Tony is pussy. He's not built for this like you."

Rodney was a monster, and so was she, so he put his gun down. Grimy recognized grimy. He knew Sharise was his kind.

"So what's in this stash?" he asked.

"About half a mill and two keys of dope," she replied.

"Ewww-weee!" Bishop said.

"And what you want out of this?"

"Half."

"You're steep."

"Well, how about this . . . You keep the two keys, and I get the money?" Rod shook his head thinking about the proposition.

"Sounds like a decent plan. Let me think on it," he said. In the back of head, he thought about how dangerous a woman scorned could be. He was grateful that Von wasn't that type of chick. She knew almost everything about him and could easily have him set up, but that wasn't in her nature.

"Before you think on it, I need an apology. You accused me of trying to set you up. What good would that do me? I'd rather align myself with the realest nicca in the city than go against him." Rodney liked the sound of that. And Sharise knew it. She was a master manipulator and a professional ego stroker.

"Okay, well, in that case, I apologize. But one can never be too careful these days." Rodney was like a vampire. He bit as many people as he could and turned them into vampires too. But he was happy to meet someone like Sharise who could match his gangster. He'd heard about her in the street, but he never tried to press her. She was known for doing low-level shit. He respected her for wanting to get dirty and play in the big leagues. He was already thinking of other ways he could use her.

"Apology accepted," she said.

"But let me warn you, I won't hesitate to chop your head off if you cross, Sharise. So please, don't cross me, baby girl." Sharise knew that Rodney was serious. She'd heard stories about him. She did not want to be one of his enemies.

"I hear you, Rod. I'll never do you dirty. That's not my style." But that was Rodney's style because he'd done her dirty already, passing his sickness right into her. Dirty was just part of his game.

CHAPTER 26

"Hurry up! Grab my bag, Paige! Oh shizzzzz-nick, these little fuggers are coming." Everybody was running around the house crazy. Von was in labor. Her water broke, and it was time to get her to the hospital.

"Okay, okay. Um, umm, Von, where is the bag?" Marla asked.

"Listen, bitch, fuck the bag. Let's go. I'm about to explode!" Von said. Marla and Paige were laughing because Von was looking like a crazy woman.

"Did you remember to call that devil?" Von asked.

"Yeah, I called Rodney. He's gonna meet us at the hospital."

"No, call him back and tell him not to come. I don't wanna see him. He's the reason I'm in all this pain right now. I don't wanna see him. Forget it. Forget it! Arghhh! Another contraction!"

"Breathe, Von! Breathe!" Paige said to her girl as they got in the back of Paige's brand-new black Maserati that

Mad-Dog bought her.

"When the hell did you get this car?" Marla asked.

"The other day."

"Damn, I'm about to ask Mad-Dog if I can be your sister wife," Marla said joking around.

"I'm glad y'all got time to joke. I ain't in no laughing mood right now!" Von said. The girls couldn't help but to laugh at Von. Von being angry was so rare, it was funny to see. They were excited to have these two new lives coming into the world. Everybody was going to meet them at the hospital. It was an exciting day.

They held Von carefully, and helped her into the emergency room. Then she was put into a wheelchair and wheeled in the delivery ward.

"How often are the contractions?" a doctor asked.

"Where is Dr. Maru?"

"She's on her way; she's stuck in traffic. But please tell me how far apart the contractions are."

"About 7 minutes or so. My water already broke." The doctor did a quick examination.

"Prep for delivery," he told the nurse, "she's ready. Who's going to be her coach?"

"I am," Marla said. "I'm her sister-in-law," she said with wishful thinking that one day Nasty would marry her.

"Okay, go with the nurse so you can get ready!"

"You'll be fine, Von. Don't worry. Marla will be right

there with you."

"Okay. Okay! I'm just nervous. I'm gonna be a mother. Just promise me you'll help me. I can't do it by myself."

"I know. And I got you."

"Before you leave, I love you. And don't let Rodney back here. I know he's gonna try. I don't wanna see him."

"I got you!" Marla walked off with the nurse to get prepped, leaving Paige and Mad-Dog in the waiting room. Then suddenly Rodney burst through the doors. He had a crazy look on his face as though he was really concerned. Maybe he was. But nobody cared about Rodney's feelings.

"Where is she?" he asked.

"She's in labor," Paige said.

"Well, I'm going up in there."

"No, you're not. She doesn't want you in there. Marla is there with her."

"How she gon' not let me see my babies born?" he asked angrily. "Who do I talk to? I know I got rights."

"She can choose her own coach."

"Man, fuck that!" He started to walk through the doors, but Mad-Dog had heard Von's request. He stood up.

"Nah, you not going back there. Not right now."

"Who da fuck you think you are, nigga? As far as I see it, you're lucky to be alive after stabbing up my brother."

"So change my luck, muh'fucka!" Mad-Dog said

putting his hand behind his back.

"Stop it! Stop it! Please, have some respect for Von. Not here, and not now."

People in the waiting room were looking at them. A few people even got up and left thinking there might be a shoot-out.

"Don't push!" Dr. Maru told Von. She made it in time and was helping to deliver the baby. Von had about eight doctors in the room. They wanted to do all they could to stop the transmission of the disease to the babies. A natural birth had the highest risk. That is the point when the mother's and baby's blood mixed. Before then, all babies have their own blood supply separate from their mother's. They needed to do a C-section, but with Von's illness, they had to be extremely careful. Her medication did not work, and Von's insides had deteriorated far worse than they anticipated.

"It hurts!" Von said.

"It's okay. Just breathe, friend!" Marla said.

"Count backward from 10," the anesthesiologist instructed. As Von counted backward, she thought about Nasty and how he would react to the letter she wrote him a few days ago. If she calculated correctly, he was reading it right now. She wondered if she said the right things to him.

Her timing was perfect. Nasty opened the letter while Von was in labor.

Dear Nasty,

Big brother, I hate that we haven't been speaking. Really, I should have come to visit you again. I was avoiding you because I was holding a secret. I didn't want you upset with me. I'm pregnant with twins. I felt like I disappointed you. I felt like I let you down. I didn't want you to be upset with me for getting pregnant by Rodney. But I am in love with my babies. And I am waiting for you to come home and help me raise them. I want you to influence them, not Rod, even though I won't deprive him of being a father. But I don't want them to be like him. I want them to be like you and Soulja. Strong with principles. So please don't be upset with me, okay? You're going to be an uncle two times over. I will bring them to see you as soon as I can. But, hey, the way things are looking, you might be home before that. Congratulations on your sentence reduction. I'm so happy. I love you.

Love,

Your Sister,

Von

Nasty read the letter and smiled. He knew his sister was pregnant. They were so close, and when he suspected it, he asked Moon to check it out. And sure 'nuff, he confirmed it. Von was as big as a house. And he knew that was the real reason she was avoiding him and not coming to visit. He was okay with it. She was a woman, and women got pregnant. He was happy to be an uncle. And he hoped that Rodney would play his role as a father. But he didn't know she was having twins. Now *that* was the real surprise.

It had been a while since Nasty smiled. He wished he could be there with her. He felt uneasy. He knew that Von was in pain. He pulled out his big box of pictures. He was searching for one in particular. He dumped the pictures on his bed and dreaded the idea of going through 500 pictures looking for one, but he had nothing else to do. Then, like magic, a strange wind came out of nowhere, and the very picture he was looking for flew off the bed onto the floor. He checked outside his cell to see if the window was open in rec. But it wasn't. Where the hell did that breeze come from? Nasty was a bit of a spook. He'd taken enough lives to know what it felt like to be bothered by a ghost.

He picked up the picture and kissed it. He thanked God for Von. She was all the good in him. The only living piece of his parents. And now that family was growing. He took a little bit of toothpaste and put it in the back of the picture of him and Von as children with their parents. Then he stuck it on the wall beside his bed. After that, he lay back and just looked at them.

Von was out cold, being cut open so her babies could be taken out. The procedure was so meticulous, the room was damn near silent when the cutting began. Marla held Von's hand. A few minutes later she heard the cry of one baby. "Oh my God! So beautiful," Marla said.

"Okay, we're taking out the second baby," Dr. Maru said. Von was out cold. Marla wished she could have been awake to see this. Then they asked Marla to leave.

"Please, just step out for a moment. The babies are out of the womb, and now we need to focus on sewing your friend up. We need the room as sterile as possible."

She felt in her heart that something was wrong, but then again, the anxiety also was coming from not knowing if the babies were infected.

"Don't worry. We are going to test them immediately. Hopefully, the disease did not transfer to them. But there is a great deal of blood in here and for your own safety, we need you to leave." Marla understood and left the room.

Tony walked through the hospital doors with cards and balloons. He loved Von like a sister. He'd known her for years. But he also wanted to impress Paige and to see Tonaya. Tonaya was sitting on Mad-Dog's lap dozing off, but she jumped up when she saw her father. She sprinted to him.

He picked up his baby. "You ready to see your little cousins?" he asked her. She nodded. Mad-Dog respected and acknowledged the bond Tony had with his daughter. The two men nodded at each other. Rod peeped it and screwed up his face. He looked at Tony, and then over at Mad-Dog, and laughed. Tony ignored him and continued to wait to be able to see the babies. Everybody loved Von.

Rodney got up from his seat and called over to Paige, "Let me holler at you for a minute." Tony and Mad-Dog glared at him. Paige got up and stepped to the side with him so they could talk in private. "I know you're upset with me and all that. I get it. But—"

"We don't have nothing to talk about, Rodney. Why is so hard for you to understand that? You know why it's taking so long back there?" she whispered. "Because Von is sick. And they have to go through all these precautions and shit. This is all your fucking fault."

"I love Von. And I'ma try my best to make it up to her."

"She don't want you!" Paige threw her hand up and walked back to Mad-Dog and sat beside him. But she was soon back on her feet.

Finally, the doctor came out. Paige jumped up. Then everyone did. "How did it go?" she asked.

"The babies are beautiful. They're both doing fine." Everybody exhaled.

"And how about Von? How is she doing?"

The doctor removed his gloves and exhaled. "Well, Dr. Maru is back there with her, and she's coming out to talk to you about Von's situation."

Everybody looked confused. They hoped that Von was all right. Only some of them knew Von was sick. So the doctor was being discreet. Then Dr. Maru emerged. A smile came across her face.

"Hello, everyone. It's nice to see Von has so much love. Von's a fighter. I loved her from the day I met her." Dr. Maru admired her support team. "I want you guys to know," she said, and then suddenly started crying . . . "that I did all I could do. We all did. But we were unable to stop the bleeding. She just wasn't strong enough. We lost her. I'm sorry. I hate to have to be the one to tell you that Von passed away."

"Excuse me? I think I misheard you," Marla said.

"I'm sorry. She's gone."

"No, no! No! I was just with her. I was just in there holding her hand and talking to her. You're a fucking liar. She's in there alive and well, ready to come home and raise those babies. Don't tell me that shit. Don't tell me that lie," Marla said with tears in her eyes and her finger pointed in the doctor's face.

Rod fell back into his seat and put his head into his hands. Reality had just gut punched him.

Paige was screaming so loud that Mad-Dog had to contain her. Tony stood there frozen and speechless. All he could do was hold onto his little girl. He wanted to console Paige, but that was Mad-Dog's job now. His heart was broken for Von and for Paige. Marla was going crazy. She fell to her knees and started praying to God that this was somehow false information. Von could not be dead. Everybody in the waiting room felt their pain. There wasn't a dry eye there. All Marla could think about is how would she tell this to Nasty. Nasty's face flashed in her mind over and over. He loved Von as if he birthed her himself. This would rip him apart. It was ripping her apart, so she knew it would destroy him.

Von watched as she walked through waiting room. She touched Paige. "I'm okay, Paige. I'm free. I'm not sick anymore. Can't you see? Please stop crying. I could have survived, but I chose this. I wanted to be free," Von said. But none of them could hear her. She kissed each of them on the cheek and told them all that she loved them.

Von then walked through the walls to her babies. She kissed both of them. They were so beautiful. They were angels, the little beings that set her free from this crazy world. Before she died, she visited Nasty. She pulled the picture of them from the bed and kissed him on his forehead.

Von was back to her true essence. An angel. She had always been one. Then she closed her eyes and ran to her parents.

CHAPTER 27

The four o'clock count cleared, and Nasty sat in his cell with a thousand things going through his mind. He'd felt strange ever since the picture had blown off his bed the way it did. The cells were unlocking. He stepped on the tier to get out of his room for a minute. He'd been inside reading most of the day, but for some reason, he could not focus. His stomach was churning, and he did not like the feeling. His heart rate was up, and anxiety had set in.

"Hey, Miller!" the guard said.

"What?" Nasty answered.

"The chaplain wants to see you!"

Now, his stomach dropped. Nasty wanted to run back to his cell and throw up. He could taste the vomit creeping up his esophagus. The feeling was not good. The chaplain meant one thing and one thing only. Death. The chaplain was supposed to represent God, but in prison, a call to go to the chaplain was like going to the chambers of the Grim Reaper.

Moments later, Nasty knocked on the door to the

chaplain's office. The wrinkly old lady stood up and opened the door. She reached out her hand and grabbed his.

"It's my sister, isn't it?" he said.

The old lady stepped back and put her head down, pulling Nasty inside. "How did you know?" she asked concerned, yet curious.

"I just knew it. I just knew it."

"I still have to confirm. Is your sister's name Shavon Miller?"

Nasty nodded in a subtle manner. The chaplain could read the wisdom in his eyes.

"I'm sorry. Yes, she's gone."

He had so much potential, and she saw that this might just ruin him. He broke down and dropped his head on her desk. Nothing in the world could be more painful, and at that very moment, he wished for death. He had no reason to live. He was upset with himself for getting up and leaving during their last visit and walking away. He should have hugged her; told her how much he loved her face-to-face. Then he thought about talking to her on her birthday and rushing off the phone to go over see a poker game he organized. He should have talked to her longer. She left without them being able to see each other.

"How did you really know? Please tell me. You were so certain!"

Nasty didn't bother to wipe his eyes; he opened the

floodgates and let it all rain down.

"She came to me today. She helped me find something I was looking for," he said sadly. Nasty's face was drenched in tears, and he could barely talk.

"What happened to her?" he asked.

"Well, I spoke with the hospital. She delivered two babies today. But she started bleeding, and they couldn't stop it from what I understand. But look at how good our Lord is. He taketh away, but he giveth. Two new lives, Mr. Miller. She had a set of fraternal twins today."

Nasty did not respond. This was all so much to deal with at one time. He got up and walked out of what felt like the chaplain's death chamber and went back to his cell, where he stayed for so long he lost count.

Everyone checked on him. All his boys. He would not come out of his room. He would not talk to anyone. Nothing in life could have prepared him for this. She missed out on the opportunity to grow with her children. To be a grandmother. To nurture them. To love them. Every time he thought about it, another piece of his heart shattered. He would soon have no heart left.

Von went out in style. Rodney made sure that she had the works. Nasty was grateful for that. So many people came out to show Von love. But Nasty heard that a big dispute broke out after the funeral about who was to keep the kids. Rod wanted the twins with his mother, but Paige was determined to carry out Von's last wishes. Von talked openly to them about if anything had ever happened to her, she wanted the babies' godparents to care for them. Rod didn't care. They were his children, and I couldn't quite blame the man. I would probably be the same way if it was me in his position.

Paige couldn't go into detail with Nasty that the real reason she didn't want the children with Rod was because he was in the same boat Von was in. Ignoring his illness, he was ignoring the children. Not caring about their future. Von didn't want that for her kids if something was to ever happen.

Von did not have a chance to name the babies. But she'd spoken often of what she wanted to name them if she had a boy or a girl. Shavon and Nameek. Those were her and Nasty's names that their parents gave them. And Paige fought like hell to make sure they were named properly. And so it was. Shavon and Nameek. She didn't want them to get Rodney's last name, but she couldn't win every battle.

It had gotten back to Nasty that the family had been giving Rod the cold shoulder. Yeah, he cheated on Von, but the girl had passed away. Nasty was sure that he was hurting inside, and he felt like the family was being harsh on Rod. She died because of a natural occurrence.

Sometimes in labor things go wrong. He had nothing to do with that, so Nasty made a mental note to talk some sense into them once the grieving calmed down some.

Nasty requested his cell phone after weeks of being silent. He called Marla.

"Baby, I've been so worried about you. You refused all my visits. I just need to know you're okay," she said.

"No, I am not okay. But I want to know how Shavon and Nameek are doing."

Marla did not have the heart or the authority to tell Nasty that Nameek was fine, but little Shavon had gotten the disease. And the doctors were waiting to see if the medicine would work for her or not. It didn't work for Von, so the chances of it working for little Shavon were slim. But the girls all held on to hope.

"Well, Shavon and Nameek are fine. We get to see them often, but Rodney and his mother filed something in court and got custody. That is not what my sister wanted, but what can I do? Unless I kidnap them, and trust me, the thought has crossed my mind." Nasty could hear the anger in her voice.

"He's their father. So at the end of the day, let that man raise his children. I will only have an issue if he tries to deprive our family of them."

"So what about us? Me and you! I'd like to see you, Nasty. We were working on something and building a beautiful relationship. I don't want this to come between us. We need each other now more than any other time. Let me love you and be there for you."

"Nah, I'm good. A relationship is not what I need right now. I'm no longer of any use to anyone." Then he hung up—just like that. Marla had to look at the phone to really make sure she wasn't imagining that he'd just hung up on her. But there was nothing but the dial tone. She knew this would destroy him, but she hoped it wouldn't destroy the love they shared. Her heart was broken all over again. First from Von, now from Nasty. Maybe the two of them really were one and the same.

Nasty's counselor called him to the office. He could not handle any more bad news. He walked in and sat down. The counselor had always been a bit of an asshole. A man named Mr. Gein.

"Mr. Nameek Miller, a.k.a. Nasty, well, the court just updated your release date. You'll be leaving in 2 weeks. Fourteen days exactly. Do you wish to be picked up?"

"What do you mean I'm leaving in 2 weeks?"

"Your two points came through, and you also got a reduction for the crack law. Looks like somebody wrote a letter on your behalf, as well, and it helped the judge make a decision. I disagree with staff getting involved and writing character letters, but it's not my business."

Nasty didn't know what this man was talking about. Staff involved? What staff member would care enough to write a character reference letter about a stone-cold killer?

Maybe it was just a rumor.

"So will you be getting picked up?"

"No! Just let me outta this bitch!" Nasty said. He signed a few documents and that was that. He had no idea this would happen so fast. It was like God was playing a foul joke on him. To give him freedom so close to Von's death. Why couldn't it have been a little bit sooner so he could have been with her? He was not excited; he felt nothing but coldness.

Nasty sat down and penned a letter to Soulja. He couldn't write him directly to another prison. So he had to send the letter to Keva so she could forward it.

My Dearest Comrade,

I write you this letter in the deepest despair. I don't know if anyone has informed you, but Von is dead. In that case, so am I. She died giving birth to my niece and nephew. I am sorry to disappoint you, brother, but you must find someone else to execute your plan. I am not the man for this. I will be home in about 2 weeks, and I can't function, knowing that my sister will not be there to greet me. This pain is too deep and too real for me to ever get over it. Love will not be there to greet me. I am in a reckless state of mind, and I cannot go on like this much longer. I hate even God himself. I am not the man to change the world. I am lost now. So please, find someone else to work the plan. Maybe the lives I took have come back to haunt me. Whatever it is, I'm going to be alone. Please don't check for me.

CHAPTER 28

Soulja walked upstairs and sat on his bed after picking up his mail. He wanted to use the phone, but he lost his phone privileges for 30 days due to making a few three-way calls. Three-way calls were restricted in federal prison. So Soulja hadn't spoken to anyone, and because he was all the way in Louisiana, he only got visits once every 90 days or so. He was happy to have some mail because he'd been out of touch for a minute and needed to know what was going on. Most of his letters had been crayon drawings from I'sa. He saved and cherished each one.

He got two letters today. One from Nasty and one from Moon. He opened the letter from Moon first, and it disturbed him. Moon explained that I'sa's teacher might be a bigger problem than anticipated. Anything regarding Soulja's daughter was a sensitive issue for him. He already had a hard time dealing with not being there to physically protect her. He did all he could do from afar. He made sure she went to a private school and lived outside of the city perimeters. He was no fool, and he knew that the business he'd been in breeds the desire for revenge. The only way to really get to Soulja was through his family, specifically, his daughter. He vowed never to let that happen.

He wasn't really worried about his mother or his other siblings because everybody in that household carried a weapon and knew how to use it. He kept a man on his house at all times for extra protection. Just in case. One could never be cautious enough. He and Nasty had done many things in their younger days that they wouldn't do now as more mature adults. So to protect his family, he made additional efforts to ensure their safety.

Moon had the teacher followed for a few weeks and hired a private investigator to do some digging into the man's background. Turns out this Mr. Rosario is related to the El Domino Cartel out of Brazil. The question was, is this a coincidence or something more?

There are hundreds of members of the El Domino Cartel. Soulja had a reputation of overreacting and jumping the gun, but he'd rather be safe than sorry. He needed more information, but his antennae were definitely up. First things first, I'sa being taken out of his class wasn't enough. He wanted her out of that school. His mind was going to murderous thoughts. So to distract himself, he opened Nasty's letter.

After reading the first line, Soulja realized something was wrong. His heart began to speed up. His eyes had turned bloodshot red. He could feel the pain rising from each and every word on the page. He could not believe that Von was dead. He had to read the letter over and over. Von?

Soulja had a different level of knowledge about Von's death than Nasty did. Soulja knew that Rodney was responsible for her death. And there was no way he was going to let him get away with murder. Soulja closed his eyes and prayed to Von asking her to forgive him because he was going to seek revenge on Rodney. It was the only honorable thing to do.

Soulja waited an excruciating 3 more days to get his phone privileges back. He called Nasty's cell phone, hoping that he had it. He didn't get an answer. But he tried all day until he got through.

"Yo!" Nasty said.

"So there is no turning back for you, huh? I got your letter, brother. I know this is the worst possible thing that could have happened. But don't throw away your future. We worked too hard. You giving up on your dreams is not going to bring Von back."

"You know me better than anybody, bro. To go on as if things are all good would be fiction. I'm numb, and how do you ignore not wanting to live anymore?"

Soulja could hear the hurt in Nasty's voice. He remembered that pain from when they were children, and Nasty showed up at his house with Von, scared to death because their parents had been found dead. He remembered the look in their eyes.

"I understand your pain. I do. But what would Von want you to do? You gotta go on, man. The children are gonna need you. You have to get through this and do what you gotta do."

"Do what I gotta do? There is *nothing* I can do."

Soulja was getting angrier and angrier that Rod had done this. He listened to Nasty speak with pain surrounding each word. Each syllable. Nasty continued, "Nothing can ease this pain, fam. What could ever fix such a loss?"

"Revenge!" Soulja said coldly. "Revenge!"

"What you mean revenge? There is nothing to avenge. My sister died because she wouldn't stop bleeding. Why would you say revenge?" Nasty asked with a recharged attentiveness.

Soulja bit down on his lip. He hated to be the one to drop the truth. If only Soulja didn't have life, he would get out and fix this problem called Rodney himself—with a vengeance that mankind had never seen before. But he had no release date. He was doing life, and he was stuck. The men were quiet on the phone.

Nasty knew that Soulja would never use the word revenge unless there was a reason. And the venom in Soulja's voice was undeniable.

"What would you say if I told you that Von may have lived if it wasn't for other complications that someone may have inflicted on her?" Soulja asked.

"I'd say, you'd be releasing the devil himself from hell and condemn many people to death," Nasty answered.

"Is that really what you would say, brother? Is that all that is important to you? I gave Von my word I would keep silent. But for the first time in my life, I will break my word if you are willing to sit still and operate under my instructions."

Nasty was hurt to hear that Von had confided in Soulja about something so serious and not him. His mind raced, and all of these crazy possibilities of what could have happened to his sister began racing through his head.

"Why did she share with you what she feared to share with me?"

"She came to see me."

"She came to see you? When were you gonna tell me this?" Nasty asked, fuming.

"Listen, she's my sister too. Maybe not by blood, but is love not a factor?"

"Man, fuck all that. So now me and you are keeping secrets from each other? What could she have said to you to make you forget your honor? To say fuck the code? They said you was getting soft, but I had your back. Maybe they were right. Because these antics right here got me questioning your integrity."

Soulja was delivering the information in a way that

suited Nasty's best interest. He was protecting him, but Nasty didn't see it that way. His grief was causing him to be disrespectful.

"I'm going to give you a pass, Nasty, due to the circumstances."

"I don't need no muh'fuckin' passes from you. I need to know what happened to my sister. I played the role as her father. Not just her brother."

"Unless you can vow to put it in on your honor that you won't move on the information you have, then I cannot give it to you. You get out in a few days. I want you to be free in a few days, not dead. So I need to know what you choose. I sacrificed my life so you could be free. I don't want you to spend your life in prison because you moved too fast. I want to tell you everything, but you have to promise me that you won't make a move outside of what I order."

"Nah, I can't promise you that. But what I can promise you is that one way or another, I will get the information I need from you or my loved ones. I no longer have a heart, so like I said, I will get the information out of you or anybody else—by any means necessary."

Soulja tried to suppress his anger. "Nasty, I love you. You have always been a brother to me. But I'm starting to think you are threatening me."

"Don't think—know! It seems that your promise to Von is more important to you than death itself. So, now, things will be done my way!" Nasty then hung up.

Soulja sat there looking at the phone in disbelief. He and Nasty had never had a fight—ever. It broke his heart. And he did not want to have to show Nasty how strategic his mind had become.

Soulja placed the phone on its hook and went back into his cell. He sat down and took out the pictures of him and Nasty and the family before any of the tragedies that brought them to this point had taken place. So much pain. So much misfortune. The game took so much from everyone.

He thought about Nasty. He loved Nasty like a brother. But everybody had a line that can never be crossed. He was in a bad mood after talking to Nasty. He hated that his man was losing his mind. His irrational thinking was turning into threats toward him and the family. He knew Nasty well enough to know that if he started making threats, he would make good on them. He was determined to find out what else went on surrounding Von's death. And to get that information, Nasty would do anything. Like he said, he no longer had a heart or a God, so nothing else mattered. Soulja did not want things to get as bad as they could get.

A few days later, Soulja got another letter from Nasty. He was outright threatening him and anybody he loved, that if he didn't get what he wanted, everybody and anybody would pay.

Would he hurt I'sa? Would he go to those depths?

Soulja was unsure. His boy was losing his mind like a rabid dog, and he did not want to have to put his man to sleep. He decided one last attempt. And he could only hope that this next scribe would make it to Nasty before he left. He decided to write him a letter and let the cards fall where they may.

Dear Brother,

 Your words came to me as a surprise. I thought that maybe you would calm down after you had a chance to think things over. But I see you wanted to further vent your frustration and anger toward me. Your threats hurt like hell. And now my heart feels two kinds of ways. And I know we know each other well enough to understand what that feeling is. I won't play these games with you. It is as simple as this: You still have a life. And I know that regardless of what you say, you value that life. A life that can be taken from you. I like to keep any war in the street, but if you don't snap out of this trance you're in, you'll end up getting smoked the day you step out of the pen. It kills me to have to speak to you this way, but you are not yourself. Don't become a victim of your own stupidity. It's as simple as that, brother. You draw first blood, and I will keep spilling it until it's over. Keep your head up. I understand your pain. But we are supposed to keep standing, even when we're down. Don't forget about 55's brother. I did that for you. I am not the enemy, and I humbly ask you not to turn me into one.

Soulja

Soulja sealed the letter and dropped it in the mailbox. He could not believe that everything had come to this. This was a new low for them. But life had a strange way of turning you upside down and inside out. As Nasty prepared for his release, Soulja prepared for possible war with his brother. Only the future could determine what would happen next.

#####

NEW TITLES FROM WAHIDA CLARK PRESENTS

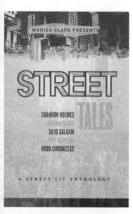

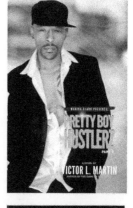

#READIT

WWW.WCLARKPUBLISHING.COM

CPSIA information can be obtained
at www.ICGtesting.com
Printed in the USA
LVHW091600080719
623438LV00001BA/25/P

9 781944 992590